BY THE NORTH DOOR

Lucy Watson, thirty-eight, plump and disorganized, scandalises her mother by marrying a man she has only just met.

She met Roland at the Marleigh Festival and, though from very different backgrounds, she becomes his wife and goes to live with him at his beautiful ancestral home, Nine Maidens. Roland is curiously reluctant to discuss his father, who had been sixty when he was born. Gradually, Lucy learns that he was said to have been a powerful magus, and the appearance of Roland's strange sister and the eerie happenings in the secret wood only add to the web of mystery surrounding the family. It might all have been too much for Lucy to handle, but then Inspector Henry Beaumont comes into the picture . . .

BY THE NORTH DOOR

Meg Elizabeth Atkins

First published 1975
by
Harper & Row, Publishers, Inc.

This edition 2006 by BBC Audiobooks Ltd
published by arrangement with
the author

ISBN 1 4056 8534 4

British Library Cataloguing in Publication Data available

Printed and bound in Great Britain by
Antony Rowe Ltd., Chippenham, Wiltshire

When one creates phantoms for oneself, one puts vampires into the world, and one must nourish these children of voluntary nightmare with one's blood, one's life, one's intelligence, and one's reason, without ever satisfying them.

Eliphas Levi

Thou shalt separate the Earth from the Fire, the subtle from the gross, gently, with much ingenuity.

Table of Hermes Trismegistus

To Peter N. Walker,
for helping me to take my first steps in crime

Prologue

THERE were occasional letters, post cards, telephone calls, communications, with the headlong quality of her smile. In her physical, accessible presence there had always been the suggestion of impermanence. People said to her, "Wait—" even when she was still. She said, "I'll stay—" but the next moment, the next hour, the next week, she was moving away, doing something else, going somewhere else. The check in the stride, the lifted hand acknowledged a desertion that was temporary, even necessary—for reasons incompletely understood by others, and by her, perhaps, not at all. The turn of the head asked forgiveness, the smile said: *I'll be back. . . .*

The last note arrived in an envelope with a postmark unreadably blurred; scribbled in her reckless hand, the note read:

> Love,
>
> I've met this man, these people; there's magic there. I'm a little apprehensive, but you know for me commitment is the only thing—even if it's for five minutes it's got to be total. So I'm going—to the house and the trees and the . . . um . . . the oblique ones. But now, for now, I can't say any more. Stay as you are, you will anyway—immovable as a rock. I'll be back.

She didn't sign her name; instead there was a curious emblem, roughly sketched and yet disturbingly complex. A series of coils crossed and interchanged with a subtle tension, leading the eye on and around and back and on again to some undiscernible, irrecoverable center. But there was about the design a line or angle or curve—too elusive to be immediately apparent—that interfered with its balance, giving an unsatisfactory impression that something must be added, or taken away, before the perfection that had been hinted at could be achieved.

That was the last letter. After that there was no word from her at all.

1

"WHAT it boils down to," Mrs. Watson said, "is if I hadn't gone away, none of this would have happened. I've never heard of anything like it: you can't marry a man you've only known five minutes. *You* can't."

"Yes, I can," Lucy said, faintly because she scarcely believed it herself. "And it's not five minutes."

Her mother, relentlessly disposing of breakfast cereal and hunting out objections, didn't listen. "At your age. I don't believe it. If I hadn't gone to Canada, if you'd come with me . . ."

"I couldn't afford it," Lucy said. "And I couldn't have two months off work, you know. And besides, I didn't want to go."

With an automatic efficiency she fried bacon, scrambled eggs, cut bread. Her small plump body was disorganized by tension, but habit held her together, directing her fine little hands. Habit had held her together for years, binding her to her mother and, with her mother, to the unvarying routine of day-to-day living. The sense of her own daring in breaking the routine, combined with the ordeal of telling her mother, produced in her a feeling of total vulnerability: she was sure that soon she would break a plate or splash the fat and be caught not caring. She might even, if she was going to spill something, contrive to spill it over her mother—which would be the ultimate in audacity, like a deliberate assault.

As she prepared breakfast, her mother's voice provided a monotonous accompaniment in the background. Mrs. Watson was a great talker; she specialized in trivialities and gave them all her attention. "It certainly wasn't as if *I* could afford to go to Canada," she said, untruthfully. "But you're under an obligation to relatives when they invite you—it was a duty, really." Lucy was familiar with the tone of martyred self-justification. At the same time, her mother claimed the trip was "a little treat I owed myself." Her life was a long indulgence of little treats, most of which she hugged to herself, the greedy pleasures of a selfish woman.

"And what about *his* relatives? You can tell a lot about people by them."

Can you? Lucy thought. Hers were dim to the point of near invisibility: respectable, predictable and boring. *Am I like that?* she thought, alarmed. *How can he love me? A man like Roland?*

"His parents are dead," she said.

"Are they? That's a good start," her mother said sarcastically. "What about the others?"

"I don't know. We haven't talked much about them," Lucy answered, apparently relinquishing defense. But she glanced at her mother, perched stiffly on the kitchen stool, and was seized by an inward gust of laughter.

... for all the world like one of those garden gnomes on a mushroom. Good God. I bet Roly-Poly can't produce one like you. I hope not.

Her mother spent a great deal of money on foundation garments and prided herself on being petite; the result was a short, dumpy body ruthlessly structured into a series of improbable curves. She wore bright clothes in styles too young, too much makeup on her round, doll-like face, and had her hair done aggressively, with a great deal of lacquer, twice a week.

I won't, Lucy promised Roland silently, with some anguish, *ever* get like that.

Unfortunately, she had a good start. The same short, plump figure, the girlishness, and something in her nature that pined for ornament, although she usually managed to resist it, having always before her the example of her mother, who had never learned where embellishment ended and vulgarity began. Roland called her his downy brown woman, because a first glimpse conveyed so much of her: her softness, her round brown eyes, her wide mouth, quick and generous. She wore her rich brown hair simply, favoring Alice bands or bows; her face was square and serious and full of expression. She had spent her life trying to understand, to sympathize, to please, and these efforts had opened out her features to an ageless, undefended look.

"You're nearly forty," her mother said scornfully.

"I'm thirty-eight," she answered patiently, knowing without vanity that she didn't look it. She pressed her age on people, eager that they should not accuse her of misrepresenting herself in any way. Roland had been astonished when she told him; he was thirty-five.

She buttered a balm cake, filled it with scrambled egg and bacon, and placed it before her mother.

"I can't eat. I'm too upset," Mrs. Watson said, attacking it with refined distaste. Then, speaking with her mouth full, "I should have known, of course, from your letters."

"But I never said anything."

"Exactly. And Mrs. Green, writing to me—"

"Her *reports,*" Lucy breathed.

"—about that Jaguar parked outside at all hours." A considering gleam showed for a moment in her eyes. "A new Jaguar, she said."

"Yes. I've told you, he's not badly off."

"Could be all show."

"It isn't. He's—he's a gentleman. His manner, his manners, his — He's really very well brought up, you can tell."

Mrs. Watson swallowed and stared. She had obsessional notions about class. "We're ordinary people, ordinary respectable humdrum people. We can't just move up the social scale on a whim. We wouldn't be accepted, unless we knew how to comport ourselves." As she said this, she took on an air of dignity so excessive and so precarious Lucy almost giggled. *Careful, you'll fall off your mushroom.*

Instead, she said firmly, "Listen, he's ordinary, too. Not humdrum. But ordinary in the way that all basically *nice* people are, however they've been brought up, or whatever their circumstances. So don't go running away with the idea that he's somehow superior to us. . . ." The advice was a waste of time; her mother, once she got hold of the idea, would run unstoppably with it among her acquaintances, to impress them. "You know, this class thing is so old-fashioned. . . ."

"Oh, I'm old-fashioned, I know I am," Mrs. Watson said strenuously, her slightly protruding eyes naked as flint. "But I'm *right.*"

Lucy poured tea. Her nature was so passive it scarcely felt the weight of domination, but beneath the yielding exterior lurked a mulish core. She had never been able to match her mother's selfishness; over the years she had managed to hold out against it by cultivating her own. "Don't you want me to be married, and happy, and have a home of my own?"

"You've got a very nice home here. What's wrong with it all of a sudden?"

"Nothing," Lucy said.

Their home was a bungalow, one of a flat road of bungalows, and apart from a brief, disastrous excursion into independence, Lucy had lived there all her life. It sat in its rigidly neat garden with a paralyzed frivolity: frilled curtains, fake shutters and a porch agog with wrought iron. Inside, overstuffed and overly cared for, it was proud of itself, lacked taste and hated people. Even the ornaments had a concussed look. She thought with a stab of utterly joyous disbelief of Roland's old house: the welcoming space and light, the incredible garden that seemed to go on forever on the aching green of new shoots, in the soft wild air of spring, down to a wood.

"Of course I want you to be happy. I just don't want you to make a fool of yourself, that's all. And going all that way away

—*if* you do. It's miles. Miles and miles."

"Not all that far, down the motorway. Three hours by car."

"Well, of course, you've been. You know. I shall just be stuck here, imagining all sorts of things. You haven't cut enough bread."

Lucy reached for the loaf. "What things?"

"How do I know, all that way away? It could be anything. Marriage is no bed of roses. And to someone you know nothing about. You're taking a big chance, aren't you? Marmalade."

"I do know about him," Lucy said. She had a direct and simple faith in all the romantic myths: marriage for her *would* be a bed of roses. She dared not say it, though, and unhappily tried to retrieve the calm she had promised herself when it came to dealing with her mother's hostility. The recollection of Roland's encouragement—*We love each other. It's two against one, darling*—didn't help. She hadn't expected her love to feel so menaced the instant it passed from her private possession.

Her mother sat rigid with indignation, waiting to be mollified. Stealing a look at the scornful, challenging face, Lucy remembered how she had been through it all before, several times, with a miserable record of apology, explanation and defeat, the sacrificial process of offering up one human being to another. She gritted her teeth. There had been too many small, spoiled dreams; Roland would not be among them.

"*What's* it called again? The place he lives?"

"Nine Maidens," Lucy murmured, for the third time.

"Well, that's ridiculous," Mrs. Watson said, demolishing it.

Stubbornly silent, Lucy put it together again: the yellowish-gray stone houses, the winding streets, the unexpected, graceful squares, the dipping lanes enclosed by trees.

Sensing resistance, Mrs. Watson returned to the attack. "And *where* did you meet him?"

"I told you. At Marleigh. At the Arts Festival."

Her mother pounced. "You didn't. Oh, no, you didn't. You said Marleigh but you didn't say anything about an Arts Festival.

What sort of thing is that? What were you doing there? It's miles."

"No, it isn't," Lucy said, marveling at her mother's obsession with distance. It must be all of a piece with not wanting anything to change, or people to do different things. *I used to be like that,* she thought. *Not now, though. Not after Marleigh.*

She had gone on an impulse, aghast at her own daring, lured perhaps by the spring that was breaking turbulently around her, overturning habit. Timid, and conspicuously alone, she had mingled with people she found eccentrically intellectual, listened to lectures she didn't understand, looked at paintings that made no sense. And met Roland. In the incandescent air there was a sense of time running away to unappeasable loneliness. Lucy, free of her mother's influence, and Roland, a stranger in a strange place, found themselves face to face in a world subtly but irretrievably altered. Their feelings took them by surprise and in a decorous panic they fell in love.

"Discussions. Paintings. Concerts." Mrs. Watson recoiled from the words as if they were personal insults. "What have you got to do with things like that? You were never strong in the upper story when it came to culture."

"There's no reason I shouldn't try," Lucy said. She had an unshakable, apologetic faith in her own stupidity, offering it to people—"I'm afraid I'm not very bright"—in the same spirit of trust and eagerness with which she offered her age. It had seemed that Roland knew everyone at the Festival. Everywhere they went he introduced her to someone—and they were all clever. She had been overwhelmed to discover that Roland "wrote things," information she dared not, at that moment, pass on to her mother. It would probably bring on a fit.

"Well, of course, if *Roland* goes in for that sort of thing, all arty and highfalutin . . ." Mrs. Watson did not add he would be capable of anything; her face said it for her. "You'll be pretty much out of your depth. We've never pretended to be a literary family."

They could hardly have cause to, the bungalow containing—from time *immemorial*, Lucy thought bleakly—nothing more stimulating than a Bible and a medical dictionary. She had never read for pleasure, having been brought up in the belief that books were idle, obscurely improper things, something to do with class.

She said, "I've never pretended anything with Roland. I don't need to. He knows all about me; I suit him as I am."

As she finished her breakfast, Mrs. Watson considered the outrageousness of it all, sometimes audibly.

Lucy washed up. (She had eaten nothing, but her mother hadn't noticed.) The kitchen had to be subdued to a state of gleaming impersonality before they left—Lucy to her work as an invoice typist, her mother to her morning job as receptionist to an optician, where she behaved with extreme superiority to people and told them unnecessarily they mustn't smoke in the waiting room. She prepared herself with little prinking motions, attracting to herself in the process rings, bracelets, earrings, scent and a shiny plastic handbag. Finally, she draped a nylon scarf over her immovable hairdo and tilted herself with genteel haste toward the door. "If I hadn't been in Canada, you'd never have done anything so daft as go to an arts festival and meet your fate."

"No," Lucy said; she thought very seriously in terms of fate. She was ready, neat in her camel coat, pulling on her supple leather gloves for driving.

"I suppose you've been letting him mess about with you, that's what it is," her mother said.

Lucy felt sick. The vulgarity of the remark, with all its degrading implications, shocked her into speechlessness. But she knew she must say something, or her mother would take it for granted the accusation was justified.

She tried to speak firmly but her voice shook a little. She had anticipated resentment and mockery and had some resources to deal with them; sustained attack was already threatening her self-command, and now, the casual coarseness that lay beneath the veneer of her mother's refinement—she had simply not expected to have to defend herself against *that.* "Must you make things sound so disgusting? My private life's my affair. I don't have to account for it to anyone."

"Well, there's nothing airy-fairy about that business, and it's what men are generally after, as you well know. I don't suppose he's any different."

"He *is,*" Lucy said, with unsteady emphasis. When she was with Roland, all the longing of her lonely, unloved body ran out to him through her voice, her eyes, her fingertips. He was courteous and gallant and restrained. He said they would wait until they were married; and she was a little ashamed, wondering why.

2

BEFORE the official work could begin, there had to be intuition, the slipping threads of memory, the uncovering of the half forgotten, its gathering and sorting.

His mind was trained. He knew how to work coolly when there was work to be done and not hamper his progress with emotional collisions. He thought slowly, writing down everything he remembered: names, places, scraps of conversation. With this flotsam and jetsam of her life, traces of her appeared and disappeared; but he went doggedly on, having always to bear in mind that in any account she gave of herself and her doings there was a margin where she lied with remarkable fluency, always with the conviction of the self-deceived. And later, disarmingly, when she had no further use for the character sustained by the lie: "Of course it's not true. I was never there. I never knew those people. I invented it all. . . ."

When he had finished, he studied the results of his efforts with minute care. Somewhere, in the mass of detail and in the unforgiving time that had consumed her, something would point to a beginning.

The unreadable postmark yielded its secret to the skill and technical resources of the GPO's investigation branch. It had been posted in Marleigh, and Marleigh was a fact; so was its Arts Festival, held every two years. She claimed to have been there several times, which was reasonable; but how much, out of those occasions, had she invented? Once, she had written:

". . .My room looks onto a garden full of weeping Victorian statuary. It's crazy. So are the people who own it; they petrified the day the British left India. . . ."

Her last letter had been posted in Marleigh, during its Arts Festival fortnight, and almost three years had elapsed since she had sent it. He thought of telephoning through to the police at Marleigh; instead, on the weekend, he drove down to the charming medieval town.

"Three years," the sergeant said. "Has she done this sort of thing before, sir?"

"All her life. She comes and goes. Nowadays the word is dropout, but drifter's probably less emotive, and nearer the truth."

"Yes, sir," the sergeant said. Certain of his superiors had charm or implacability; occasionally, like Inspector Henry Beaumont, they combined both. And this man had another quality, something the sergeant would have found impossible to describe but which, in some unreachable fastness of his imagination, he likened to a panther. He asked, "Why now?"

"Because it's been too long. After a couple of years at most there's always been some word about her, if not from her. And . . . intuition." Henry used the word without any trace of apology; intuition, in a good policeman, was the sense that supplemented the other five.

"Right. What can you give me?" the sergeant asked.

"Very little, I'm afraid. A photograph. A couple of names of people she associated with, maybe only during Festival time; I can't be sure of that. A description of a place she might have stayed at, visited, been known at. Not much, I know, even if this was official. As it is . . ." He didn't need to tell the sergeant his job. This was the problematical business where patience and chance would turn something up, where his men, in the course of their official work, would come upon a connection.

The sergeant studied the names Henry had given him. "You've tried Criminal Records?"

"Nothing there. I didn't expect there would be. Her element is the unconventional, not the criminal."

The irony in Henry's voice made the sergeant pause, but only for a moment. "You would know?"

"Oh, I'd know."

"Good," the sergeant said doubtfully. This woman could appear and disappear like a cork bobbing about on the sea; she could misrepresent herself, her doings and her acquaintances; she could vanish from sight entirely, anchored to reality only by some fanciful description of where she might have been, and yet . . . she retained her innocence in the mind of this hard man.

He should know better, the sergeant thought reproachfully, despairing of the irrationality of human emotion.

From time to time, Henry telephoned Marleigh, although he knew he would be informed as soon as anything turned up that would be likely to interest him. And from time to time, on weekends, he drove down, his hunting instinct impelling him to cover the ground himself.

At last, a young detective constable, investigating a burglary at one of the stately houses off the square, glanced into the garden next door and remembered something. When he went back to the station, he said to the sergeant, "You know that inspector from up north? Missing persons inquiry? Wasn't there something about statues in a garden?"

The house looked much too respectable to contain her. The hall gleamed with Benares brass, and antlers started from the walls. The woman in Shetland knitwear and sensible shoes said, "Goodness, no, she never *stayed* here. We have our own friends during the Festival, people of considerable standing in the cultural world, not . . . er . . . fringe people. We do hold soirees, of course, and the young ones especially are inclined to drift in and out, they're so informal. Has she done something frightful? I wouldn't be surprised; she had such an impetuous air—not that there was any harm in her." She handed the photograph back to Henry and said with great severity, "Tea?"

"Thank you."

She dealt with the china tea service as if it had in some way misbehaved itself; but in the great, empty house her days were long and had hardened into silence. Company softened her. Although Henry dressed too well and was obviously not a gentleman, his diffidence and subdued good manners allowed her to treat him as an equal. He conversed easily and was an attentive listener; his questions seemed merely polite punctuations to her monologue.

"Perhaps your husband might remember something else?"

"Reginald died six months ago," the woman said, very firmly.

"I see. I'm sorry."

"Thank you," she said, for a few moments looking beyond him, steadfastly, into nothing. "She called herself Smith. Just that, nothing else. One was bound to remember. I asked her if she was related to the Calcutta Smiths and she said naturally. Was she?"

He choked with laughter on a Bath Oliver biscuit. "I don't think . . ."

"No, I must confess I don't either. Although they were inclined to be strange."

"Did you know who she stayed with?"

"Friends of my nephew, I believe. He has extremely liberal views; it must be very difficult for him to make up his mind on important subjects. They lived "—her hand went out in a quelling gesture to the window—"over there."

Henry crossed the room and looked out. Beyond a wall stood a line of tall houses, their backs overlooking the shrubs and statuary of her garden. Some of the houses had a makeshift look and curtains that did not match, a general air—not of neglect—of incoherence.

"Of course," he said. "Flats. Bed-sitting rooms."

"The neighborhood's going down frightfully. She stayed at one of those houses; I'm afraid I don't know which one. I remember her pointing it out to Reginald once. She said she could see our garden from her window. The people—I'm frightfully sorry, the name escapes me—used to let rooms. All the year, not just at Festival time."

"Used to?"

"They've gone. Last year. I don't know where. My nephew might. Unfortunately, he's in Madrid at the moment. But you could go round and ask. The same tenants could still be there, I suppose. Bore for you, though."

Henry smiled. "I'm used to it."

The attic was warm and the light hard, mercilessly exposing the scarred suitcase, its meager contents. Henry said, "She left this? Only this? You're sure?"

"Absolutely." The young man sat by the door on a wooden chest, hugging his knees. "Beryl and Bill said they'd keep a few things for her, when she went off that year. She said she'd come back for them, or send somebody, but she never did."

"You were living here then?"

"Yes, we had the middle floor. Then, when we decided to buy the house, just as it stood, with everything in it . . . well, her case was still here. We just left it. It wasn't doing any harm. Besides . . ."

"Besides, what?"

"She didn't have much; there might have been something in

there she needed. Although she didn't seem to need much. I always thought of her as one of those people who float over the surface of life. Here we all are, tying ourselves down with jobs and permanent relationships and God knows what else—and there she is, just out of reach, dreaming, doing crazy things, finding happiness in the weirdest corners."

"Such as?" Henry said, very still.

The young man shrugged. "Oh, I don't know. Just an impression. I didn't *know* her. I can honestly say I never even had a conversation with her. I always meant to, but somehow she was . . . as I said, just out of reach. And it was such a long time ago —four years now."

"You didn't see anything of her during this last Festival."

"No. I haven't set eyes on her since the time before. And then it was only glimpses—on the stairs, going in and out, that sort of thing. And then she . . . well, she just wasn't here anymore."

"That was when the Festival ended?"

"Mm. Yes, it would be."

"Did anybody say anything about where she'd gone? Who she'd gone with?" When the young man responded with an apologetic shake of the head, Henry persisted. "Think of the last time you saw her. Tell me about it."

The young man sat silent for some moments, frowning. His expression cleared suddenly. "Oh, yes, of course. I was coming in, up the front steps—you know how wide they are—and she was across from me, going down them, towards the square. She was alone. There must have been some people in the porch because she turned back, only for a minute. I saw her face in the lamplight; it was excited, as if she was going somewhere special."

"Lamplight. She turned back. What was she wearing? Carrying? You're sure she was alone?"

"Yes. Carrying? A small case, I think. It was difficult to see because it was dark, and raining, and she was wearing a cloak. When I think of it, it was like a scene from a film, just one scene that sticks in your mind out of all the hundreds of films you see.

The streets shining with rain, her figure in that dramatic cloak, just poised on the step for an instant as she turned. And the lamplight was on her face, and she said, 'I'll be back. . . .' Yes, I'm sure she said that. I hope so; it fits with the scene, doesn't it? But she never did come back, and that fits, too, somehow. I'm not even sure why."

"You mean," Henry said slowly, "that the last time you saw her was the last time anyone saw her in Marleigh? In other words, she left that night."

"She must have. I never even knew I knew that. It was before the Festival ended—just. Some people stay the whole fortnight, others come and go all the time. It's like a series of seismic disturbances."

"It must be." Henry went to the wooden chest and perched on the edge of it, offering a cigarette to the young man. His voice was quietly encouraging. "The scene from the film: think of it again, have another look at it in your mind. The colors, the rain . . ."

"All the colors of nighttime: blues, grays, some silver—that was the rain, I suppose. And her cloak, sweeping round her, very black . . ."

"She turns. You see her face. She says, 'I'll be back,' and lifts her hand. . . ."

"Yes. Then she goes away, quickly, smoothly along the pavement, to . . ."

"Someone waiting? A car?"

"There's always a line of cars parked along this road. I don't think . . . I must have stopped looking then. Yes. Someone else came out of the house, and said something to . . . Who was on the porch? Um . . . Beryl and Bill. Bill said, 'Festival weather.' It *always* rains, nearly the whole bloody fortnight. And we agreed it was bound to clear up the next day because it was all more or less over, and—" He stopped and stared wonderingly at Henry for a moment. "I looked again. Of course I did. She was at the corner, and there was a car, and a woman. Tall, very slim, with long, pale hair. How did I know it was pale? Must have been the lamplight again."

"You didn't know her?"

He shook his head. "I'd scarcely recognize her at that distance, and only a glimpse. Unless I knew her very well. But I didn't."

"The car?"

"No. I'm not a car man; they all look the same to me. The only distinction I make is that some are big and some are small."

"This one?"

"Big. I think."

Henry nodded. He thought for a moment and then returned to the suitcase, kneeling beside it on the wooden floor.

There were some clothes, their musty smell hanging lifelessly on the air. As he examined them, a wisp of perfume moved vagrantly for a moment and was lost. A small package containing needles and thread and a pair of scissors; a flashlight; a tube of suntan lotion; a woolen head scarf wrapped around something. Carefully he unwrapped it and found a book.

The book was in a dilapidated state, its black leather cover loose at the joints, and several of the pages, which had the expensive, grainy quality of handmade paper, were loose, some of them torn. The title page announced the book to be *The Fifth Element: an exposition of the secret doctrine of the Great Mage Aleph.* The gold lettering along the spine read simply *The Fifth Element,* and beneath it was an emblem, also tooled in gold. The emblem appeared again on the front cover, this time worked in inlaid leather: a flexible, coiling design, beautifully coherent, mysterious in its vanishing sense of completeness.

He recognized it instantly, but with the nagging sense that something was different. It was the same emblem with which she had signed her last letter.

LUCY had thought in terms of stamping her personality on the house—the suggestion might even have been Roland's—but at the critical moment she discovered she had no personality. "Where shall I begin?" she asked. "Anywhere you like, little Lucy," Roland said, patting her hand and going away.

Space defeated her. It seemed constantly to be rearranging itself in the many rooms, the turns of the corridors, the doors forever opening out onto garden or yard. The house was built on the site of a twelfth-century abbey community that had fallen into disrepair at the time of the Dissolution. There had been many depletions and additions; time had worked, wrecking or reorganizing or simply rubbing softly away. Many of the original buildings of the community still stood, scattered around the wood and by the river and down into the little town. Some of the stones of the house itself were so old Lucy could not reconcile herself to the thought they were safe. She discovered, with horror, that one section of the building had, in fact, disappeared entirely, five years previously. "But that was a fire," Roland said, laughing at her.

"Oh, my God," Lucy said. "D'you mean it just catches fire by itself?"

"No, of course not. It was just a part of the house that jutted out, mostly wood. That was what made it a hazard."

She thought he dismissed hazards very nonchalantly. "You're awfully brave. What happened?"

Roland had been reading, wearing his spectacles. The afternoon light glazed the lenses, making his face blind. "My father used to use that part; sometimes he did chemical experiments. It wasn't safe, really. He was old, and he made mistakes. We tried to dissuade him, but there was something he wanted to do. He was alone, and with naked lights and the kind of stuff he was handling . . ."

"Was that how he died?" Lucy asked in a low voice.

"No. Oh, no. He got out. But the place was an inferno; nothing inside could be saved. He'd been very ill for a long time; he died shortly afterwards."

"Oh," Lucy said, softly and inadequately. For a moment there was a note in Roland's voice she couldn't define; it unnerved her. And his face, with the light blanking out his spectacles, was the face of a stranger. She got up and went across the long, low-ceilinged room to sit beside him. She was accustomed to rooms so full of furniture they were like obstacle courses. Here the space made her conscious of her plumpness and the busy forward tilt of her body. She wouldn't for one minute have wished herself back in her mother's overstuffed bungalow, but she did wish she could feel less exposed and, occasionally, be graceful.

She squeezed into Roland's armchair, snuggling up to him. He smiled, patted her knee and returned to his book. "Never mind your silly book. Talk to little Lucy."

"What about?" he asked, smiling, his eyes still on the page.

"Tell me about your father." His relatives were annoyingly elusive; they all seemed to be dead, or living abroad, or out of touch. She did want to pin one of them down. It might make her feel that her marriage had slightly more reality than the magazine stories in which people lived happily ever after.

"He was a book dealer, like you," she prompted. "And was he a writer, too?"

"He was a remarkable man."

Lucy waited for something else, eventually saying, "He must have been, to have a Roly-Poly like you."

"You mustn't listen to any stories people might try to tell you when you talk to them."

She almost said, *I don't talk to anyone.* Tradespeople, cheerful good mornings, lovely days to neighbors glimpsed as she went in or out . . . She was longing to make friends. Roland was so self-contained he didn't seem to need any. "I won't," she promised. "What sort of stories?"

"People will say anything," he answered, with an uncontrolled note that touched savagery. Then he patted her knee and began to talk normally. "He spent most of his life in the East; his money was in rubber plantations. He didn't marry till late in life, then he came here; this house, in fact, belonged to his first wife. She died, and he married again, my mother. Of course, she was much younger than he was; in fact, when I was born he was sixty. She died when I was five. His great interest was old religions, mysticism, the supernatural. He was associated with all the movements—the Golden Dawn, the Rosicrucians, the Order of the Templars of the Orient. He never made an exhibition of himself, courting publicity the way some of them did. It was his life's work, developing his magical self. He acquired great knowledge and had powers some of those charlatans couldn't begin to understand."

Lucy struggled with the feeling that Roland was telling her something that was not quite true. He had often said to her, "I'm an ordinary sort of chap," and she had agreed, because the sense of his being comfortable and moderate, even in some respects a little like herself, was what made her so much at ease with him. Now, from his ordinariness, he produced an outrageously exotic parent, an old man who was devoted to the occult, sired children at sixty, and almost succeeded in blowing himself up in dangerous experiments when he was well into his eighties. If those were the facts, what could anyone possibly tell her that would cause Roland's disapproval?

"Do you mean he was . . . er . . ." Definition escaped her; she was completely at a loss.

"A magus, the highest magical grade."

She sat up, away from him, a little stiffly. She had lost all thought of being kittenish. "Roland, you don't seem . . . How can you be so matter-of-fact? I mean, it's a bit unusual, isn't it?"

"Not if you're brought up with the idea."

"No, I suppose not." Disconcerted, she got up and wandered about. "There aren't any more of you, are there? Brought up with the idea, I mean. Brothers or sisters?"

"No."

He turned his attention back to his book. She stayed where she was for a while, looking at him, then she went out.

The house was enclosed by bushes and trees that shut out any immediate view of their neighbors or the road. Its charm was its rough, uneven disposition of stone, different angles and textures, the changes in the level of the ground. At the side of the house, the portion of the building that had remained after the fire had weathered and become overgrown with climbing shrubs. Slabs of stone that might have been the original floor, or pieces of collapsed wall, were bedded into the ground. Grass and small plants grew softly between the slabs, claiming back what had been discolored or destroyed.

Lucy stood looking about her. She would have liked to know more, details that would push out the narrow limits of her imagination, but something in Roland's manner discouraged questions. Perhaps he was still grieving for his father; it would be understandable. A man so remarkable would leave an enormous gap in the lives of people close to him. Something turned in her mind: Roland saying, "We tried to dissuade him." *We.*

She trod carefully on the slabs of stone and traced with her hand the blocks that rose steplike, tangled with honeysuckle, to join the body of the house. She made a silent apology for her presence, her curiosity: *It's only because I love him, I want to know all about him. You don't mind, do you?*

In the bird-hung stillness of the afternoon, something made her turn her head, something that touched the edge of her attention and dissolved even as she wondered what it was. She looked about the silent yard. The dense gold of the sun painted the air around her, fastening everything to immobility. Through the archway where the garden lay, not a breath moved the foliage.

An unaccountable anxiety stirred in her. She felt impelled to move away and walked slowly toward the archway and beneath it.

The garden was very beautiful, sweeping in a profusion of colors and textures, utterly unlike the bungalow garden, where the ruthless regimentation of bulbs in spring had alternated with suppressed clumps of annuals in summer. And it was large. Everything in Lucy's new life compelled her toward action by providing the space where she could exercise it; but she did not know what to do. She could rearrange the house or the garden as she pleased, and the mere idea of doing either of those things made her lost. She knew she would force herself, she knew the desire to impress something of herself on her perfect, passive surroundings would take hold of her, occupy her—save her.

She stood motionless, blankly surveying the golden cascades of laburnum. Despair moved treacherously beneath her self-deluded, accessible happiness, threatening to engulf her.

Why was Roland so different?

She struggled with notions of disloyalty, the awful echo of her mother's warnings—How can you marry him? You don't even know him—and found the stubbornness to justify herself.

Of course she knew Roland. At least, she had known the Roland of the Festival, the assured and rather dashing man, so much at ease with so many people, who cherished her timidity and took pleasure in her lack of affectation. The conversion of this Roland into the Roland who courted her was so gradual she was scarcely aware of change. His boyishness increasingly complemented her naïveté, his ardor apologetically capitulated to her conventions. The shyly romantic Roland who suggested marriage by special license evolved yet again, untraceably; by the time she married him he had solidified into respectability and in his comfortable, commonplace way he was the ideal husband for her.

The shifts and changes of a character in which nothing seemed constant bewildered her. "Every day I find out something new about you," she complained, very prettily, so that he should not be offended. What she meant was that every day she knew less about him. All the Rolands were at present contained in him, but in such small quantities they were scarcely discernible. There was now a remoteness about him; it was as if his entire personality had been erased and he was waiting to begin again.

Disturbing thoughts haunted her as she wandered alone in the garden—fears of being let down, cheated, deluded by her own romanticism. She refused to examine her fears, diverting them to sensible advice to herself that she had everything a girl could wish for (once reconciled, her mother had also claimed that for her, with dreadful swank, to anyone who would listen). It was only a matter of time. Every newly married couple went through a period of adjustment, of waiting.

Waiting . . . that word again, stealing upon the boundaries of the comfort she sought. Impatiently, she shook away her uneasiness. *I'm just a silly, nervous bride*, she thought. The image pleased her; it invested her with an appealing frailty. She gave herself up to it and went back into the house.

Roland had gone into his study, where he sat writing at his desk. He didn't like to be disturbed, but Lucy needed to cast herself upon his indifference. "I feel lonely, Roly-Poly. I feel lost. I can't seem to get used to being here. It's not that I don't love you; I do, terribly. But somehow you're different."

Imperturbably, he denied this; he had been claimed by his limitless, untenanted life, where everything was in suspension. Lucy wondered why she had not noticed before a certain physical change: he was not a big man but neatness had somehow contracted, giving him a compact wariness that went with the anonymous look of a man whose thoughts were turned watchfully inward.

Would he—she asked anxiously—go into town with her? She couldn't make up her mind about the new curtains and coverings; he could look at patterns with her, help her choose. Or kitchens, things for kitchens; he had said she could redo the rather old-fashioned one as she pleased but she wanted to know what would please him. "I feel I might do something wrong, doing it by myself. I haven't got many ideas. I haven't got any ideas. I don't even know if I've got much taste. My mother did everything at home, and you know what that was like."

For an instant she had reclaimed him. "Oh, God, yes," he said, awe-struck. "I never knew you could get so much stuff in one house. And all of it looked stunned."

"It was; it was all that dusting and cleaning and polishing. Things were just targets, really. Including me. You've given me so much." She stood behind him, her hands on his shoulders, bending to put her cheek against his hair. "I've only come alive since I've known you." She wanted that so much to be true she really believed it.

He patted her hand. "But you go, Lucy. I'm busy. You don't need me."

"We need each other. Marriage is a partnership, a sharing, a togetherness. . . ." She loved words like "togetherness," she believed in them, it was part of her charm; but she put too much faith in them, and was constantly betrayed.

"Of course it is," he said, unreachable in agreement. "And we've got each other."

They had; there was nothing more to be said. She changed tactics. "Shall we invite some people in for drinks?"

"If you like. Which people?"

"Well . . . people round about. I mean, I see them, I say good morning, but I don't know them. I think it's important to be on good terms with neighbors, don't you?" He made a noncommittal sound and a fugitive irritation stirred in her. Her generous mouth turned down, disappointed as a child's. "Or isn't it done? I wouldn't know. I'm so suburban, aren't I? I mean, where I lived everyone knew everyone else. We couldn't get away, really, because we could *see* each other, in our gardens or going in and out.

You could see who had new curtains and new clothes and a new car, and people *talked* and watched what you were doing, and you watched them. . . ." Her voice had become unsteady, a shrillness running away with words she hadn't meant to speak. He turned in his chair, took her hand gently and squeezed it. She stopped talking and pressed her fingers over his, clinging to him. "I'm sorry, Roland."

"Do you miss that, Lucy? Have I taken you away from things that matter to you?"

"Oh, no, no—you're all that matters to me. But I'm a bit out of my depth, socially, I mean. I don't want to do the wrong thing. I thought people who lived in places like this were always having drinks in each other's houses."

"Well, not all the time," he said, smiling at her. "Or they'd qualify for Alcoholics Anonymous."

She gave a stifled giggle. "Yes, wouldn't they? Shall I, though? Invite the neighbors?"

"Whenever you like," he said, squeezing her hand again, this time with the air of humoring her.

"And your friends. We'll ask your friends."

"I don't mix much."

I know, she thought bleakly, looking about the charming, book-lined room. This seemed to be all he needed: books, what he could read in them, what he could write about them, how he could buy and sell them; incomprehensible telephone conversations with fellow dealers; mountainous mail concerned with incunabula, private presses, first editions, limited editions, mysteriously designated by such terms as "Crown 8vo uncut top edges gilt, nice"; days at auctions, days in shops, miles of travel to look at collections. How could he have time for friends?

Everyone had friends. Lucy herself had several; she had never liked them very much and left them behind with scarcely a thought, but all the same they had served the purpose of filling out her world with the trivial shift of talk and interest.

"Isn't there anyone you'd specially like to invite?" she asked wistfully.

"No," he said, promptly.

There could only be one reason, she thought, giving way to secret anguish. He was ashamed of her. She was provincial and empty-headed and his friends would laugh among themselves and wonder why he had married her. So did she, sometimes.

4

SHE went into town, bravely, in her new car and pretended to be busy, and after that day she went many times without trying to persuade Roland to go with her.

She occupied herself in an unadventurous way with the house, moving a table here, a chest there, replacing anything worn or superannuated. The house was too perfect, too graceful in its proportions and its contents for her to attempt anything in the way of improvement. She took classes in flower arranging and dressmaking and joined the local gardening club. When anyone suggested a new interest to her, she clutched at it as if it were a life line to save her from drowning.

She sought company wherever she could, taking her apologetic eagerness to the fringes of other people's lives. She held coffee mornings and tea parties to which she invited women who—without exception—had clear, assured voices and perfect marriages. She introduced them shyly to Roland and referred to them often as her friends, knowing perfectly well that if she disappeared before their eyes they would scarcely notice and never miss her from their smart, socially competitive world.

Whenever she could, she dragged Roland's father into conversations, asking people if they had known him. Reactions ranged from the blankness of new arrivals who had heard nothing, through embarrassment and strangled credulity, to unashamed fascination. She often felt herself to be the object of curiosity, even interest, but the interest waned when it became obvious that she could add nothing to the fund of local gossip. Her guileless, persistent questions bored people, her lack of tact embarrassed them. Eventually, an outspoken neighbor gave her some advice. "Lucy, you really shouldn't wave that mad father-in-law of yours about like a banner; everyone's completely brassed off with him. It might be different if you knew if he really could turn people into frogs, or something, but you don't. And your husband obviously doesn't tell you anything because you're such a silly chatterbox. *Does* he talk to you about him?"

"No," Lucy whispered, overwhelmed by the headmistressy manner.

"No, we thought not. Well, he's hardly the kind of relative you'd want in a well-regulated family. Just let the old boy rest in peace, there's a good girl. Why don't you take up riding? It'll give you something to do, and you could be ready to hunt by November."

"No, thank you," Lucy said. "I'm afraid of horses."

She went home humiliated, resolving never to speak of her father-in-law again. She began to hate him, at first for the immediate reason that he had been the cause of her making a fool of herself. But her hurt went deep, and once she had admitted it, she discovered, lurking beneath the apparent, another reason. It was his influence that had changed Roland. His influence, baleful and penetrating, that had removed the boyish, ordinary, ardent Roland—all the Rolands who had been accessible to her love. She couldn't tell Roland. He was kind to her, generous, indulgent to her busy, trivial interests; but a sense of separateness hung between them, and her hurt was locked inside herself, with another pain she dared not release.

She kept to the house for some days, pretending to be out of sorts. Roland was concerned, waiting on her with endearing clumsiness—he could do nothing about the house without creating chaos. He suggested a doctor, a new dress, friends to visit. "No," Lucy said wildly. She couldn't bear to see anyone. She felt they were all laughing at her, despising her for a silly, vulgar woman. She sat about, hoping to look fragile and trying not to let the thought of her late father-in-law make her hysterical, until the sound of Roland dropping things in the kitchen drove her to pull herself together. She took up her ineffectual potterings about the house once more and ventured into the garden, where she felt conspicuous, although she knew no one could see her. Then one day when Roland was out, she went down into the cellar to look for some gardening tools.

Beneath the house, the connecting rooms of the cellars had the dry, whispering air of places seldom used. Vagrant sunlight filtered from oddly placed windows onto an accumulation of objects. In some rooms there was no direct light, only a naked bulb, shrouded in dust and interlaced by drifting streamers of derelict cobwebs. She had not explored the cellars; their contents had all the allure of the unexpected. She searched for plant pots and twine and packs of compost, knowing that when she moved something dozens of minute, secret creatures scurried for the safety of crevices. She was too interested to be frightened—so long as nothing ran up her leg—and kept her thoughts resolutely turned from mice.

As she went on, she fell under the spell of the aimless pleasure of moving things simply to see what was behind them. Pieces of furniture, pictures, packing cases, bundles of paper, books, books, books. She delved about, busy as a squirrel, diverted into wondering what things were, who had used them, who had saved them. When eventually she had found what she wanted she paused, her throat dry with dust, and looked at the wall in front of her.

"Well, that's that," she said briskly, and the moment her words died, the silence seized her.

She stood tautly in the arrested act of dusting her hands together. The air shifted, as if its density had increased and was shutting down on her, breathing a chill over her bare arms and legs and the nape of her neck.

She was staring straight ahead, at the wall, straining to see in the dim light of the bulb over her head. In one corner, forming the angle of the room, the texture of the wall changed to rough plasterwork. She followed the shape of it with her eye: up, across, down. Only gradually did she realize that what she was looking at was a rectangle framed by wood, the wood itself not entirely obscured by plaster.

Some impulse she didn't understand made her reach out, her arm heavy in the strange pressure of the air. She touched the wood, tracing the half-concealed designs carved upon it.

Some plaster dislodged, floating weightlessly, without sound, dissolving into the dissolving stillness and gathered into darkness at her feet. The outlines of the carvings were transmitted through her fingertips, faintly at first, and then more and more strongly, until a fluid, intricate movement engrossed her. She had a helpless sense of being drawn through invisible boundaries, coiling and coiling, while images just beyond her vision slid and merged, gliding a phantasmagoric measure to unheard music. She had a confused experience of the air beginning to vibrate, gathering to a whirling force, receding to a point of light—a pinprick in space—that suddenly, fatally, rebounded, streaking toward her on a swordlike brilliance.

She cried out, wrenching her hand away and leaping back, colliding with simple, homely objects whose noise fell about her, snatching her back to reality. She turned and ran, clumsy and gasping, through the cellars, flinging herself up the flight of steps by which she had entered, and out into the sunlit garden.

She had traveled an unmeasurable distance down the road. No one was about; the world had become depopulated, increasing her sense of nightmare. Her neighbors' houses were widely spaced, remote in their lush, slumbering gardens; with a curiously distracted determination she tramped up drives, knocked on doors, turning away at last when there was no answer and going on to the next house. She tried four. At one gate an enormous dog growled at her and she was too afraid to go in. She saw a car turn off the road ahead of her and go bumping down a narrow lane. She followed it at a panic-stricken trot until it stopped in front of the gates of a pretty white house. A woman got out, wrestling with parcels. Lucy advanced on her, crying with strident brightness, "Hello. I'm your neighbor, Lucy Deane."

"Good afternoon," the woman said, disconcerted. She grabbed at a capsizing shopping bag and Lucy dived to help her.

"I haven't been here long. I mean, I haven't been married to Roland very long, and there are so many people I don't know. I thought I'd just pop in and say hello as I was passing." Lucy spoke rapidly, picking up tins and paper bags of food and dropping them again. The woman retrieved them, regarding her with remote disbelief. Lucy's gardening dress was grubby, her hair wild, her startled, helpless face streaked with dirt.

"How kind," the woman murmured. "Are you all right? You haven't been out in the sun without a hat, have you?"

"Yes. Yes, I have. I've been in the sun *quite some time.* Gardening. I do a lot of gardening. Generally, I don't wear a hat. I don't think I actually have a hat. . . ." The awful possibility that she might have dropped an *h* somewhere made Lucy stop talking.

The woman was large and elegant. Her obvious astonishment was contained by her dignity. Her voice had the beautiful, assertive tone that always made Lucy feel insignificant and badly behaved. "I hope you'll forgive me. I'm a little occupied at the moment for social calls. Some other time . . ."

"Oh, God," Lucy said. "Oh, God, you must think I'm mad. There's no one in the house. I've had a—a frightening thing happen. I just wanted to talk to someone."

"I see. Well, I'm Ruth Drake. Do you want me to phone the police?"

"Oh, no, it was nothing like that. Not someone, just a sort of something."

"Deane, did you say? You live at the white house?"

"Yes."

"Of course. Well, come on in. I'll give you a drink. I think you need one."

"I don't usually do things like this, just running up to strangers. I hope you don't think I'm silly. . . ." So many people seemed to, Lucy might almost have added, her mouth trembling with the aftereffects of shock and self-pity.

"Not at all. I did see you in the car mirror, following me down the drive, and I must admit I thought you might be selling something. But you're not, so that's all right." Ruth Drake had a bracing air of common sense, softened by a hint of sympathy. Capably dealing with parcels and keys, she opened the door of her neat little house and drew Lucy in. "Now, come and tell me all about it."

The outside door of the cellar was recessed, absorbed into its own moist shadow. The colors of the afternoon stood about it, brilliant and scented. Lucy waited well away from the door, claiming her place in the sun. The brandy she had drunk had made her light-headed and her anxieties disorganized her. At last she heard footsteps from the cellar and she began to call out, peering down the dark well of the steps. "Are you all right? Is everything all right?"

Ruth Drake rose emphatically to view, obviously unmolested by any experience, real or imagined. Not even the cobwebs had dared to attach themselves to her. "Nothing, I'm afraid," she said, with a trace of regret that made Lucy marvel.

"You're terribly brave."

"Not at all. Just deeply interested."

"You found the place?"

"Undoubtedly." Efficiently, she stowed away in her handbag the flashlight she had had the forethought to bring. She had a considering note to her voice and spoke in an absorbed way, as if her intention was not to communicate anything to Lucy but simply to order her thoughts. "Obviously a door. Obviously sealed in a considerable time ago. I picked away some of the plaster from the wooden frame—"

Lucy gasped at such boldness.

"I didn't do any damage," Ruth Drake said, misinterpreting the reaction. "I just uncovered a little more of the carvings. There are some worked into the stone as well, above the door, you know. They're extremely interesting; talismans, it would seem. Now, I think I have the geography right, but to orientate myself exactly I suggest we go round to the side of the house."

"What?" Lucy said blankly.

"The portion that was destroyed by fire. You must show me," Ruth said authoritatively. She looked at Lucy, standing bewildered and useless, and added, "My dear."

"Yes," Lucy said. Kindness served to make her eager. She led the way, trotting beside the firmly striding Ruth. "Would you mind telling me why? Is it important?"

"Crucial. I'm surprised you haven't worked it out for yourself. It was his territory—not merely the part at ground level that was burned down, but *underneath*, as well. I suppose he could approach it from the house; outside, perhaps. Definitely from the inside, through the cellar. The door that's filled in now, you see, was an entrance to a corridor, I fancy, even an anteroom, a flight of steps—"

"Oh, God. Him again," Lucy said, halting.

Ruth went purposefully on. She was not to be put off by Lucy's whims. She spoke over her shoulder, drawing Lucy on to follow her. "My dear girl, it's been patently obvious, practically from your first words, that all this is relevant to the magus. I couldn't help noticing that you seem reluctant to name names: a primitive fear, understandable in one unfamiliar with such matters. I think I'm absolutely right in assuring you that there's nothing to be afraid of."

"It's not that. Entirely," Lucy said. "Well, here we are." She gestured about her. "There's nothing much to see. It's all grown over now."

"Quite. But we are walking about on the spot," Ruth said, demonstrating in her large, expensive shoes, "directly above the source of your contact. Now, was there a door here, I wonder. . . ." She began an enthusiastic examination of the wall, separating the curling, sweet-smelling tendrils of honeysuckle.

Standing once again in the heat of the sun, with the scorched paving burning through the soles of her thin sandals and the beginnings of a headache threatening to add to her distress, Lucy was humiliatingly aware of being redundant. She asked, "What do you mean . . . contact?" She did not much like the sound of the word but had to assert herself somehow.

Ruth paused and looked at her carefully before answering. "I don't know if you are one of those people who admit the possibility that certain phenomena can't be accounted for rationally, scientifically. I class myself as a skeptic, it's not easy to pull the wool over my eyes; however, I keep an open mind. Some things, ESP, precognition, operate in areas we don't fully comprehend. If we seek an explanation for them, we must first make the intellectual adjustment of admitting their possibility."

Wide-eyed, Lucy nodded. Ruth resembled—both physically and in manner—the superior woman who had called Lucy a silly chatterbox. But because she was now being treated with respect, Lucy felt obscurely she had scored a victory. She didn't entirely understand what Ruth was talking about, but it was flattering to be treated as if she might.

"I see you agree. Good. You will, of course, concede that certain people are born with gifts, powers beyond the normal."

"You don't mean me—feeling that in the cellar when you didn't?" Lucy said, half thrilled.

"Certainly not. I mean your late father-in-law."

"Oh."

"How much do you know about him?"

"I . . . er . . ." Lucy looked away. "I still don't see where the contact comes in."

Ruth almost sighed, restraining herself by a stiff smile. "The late Mr. Deane was a remarkable man. He undoubtedly had great psychic gifts and an astonishing knowledge of magical lore. It was said that after a lifetime of study he perfected a formula whereby he could achieve an indefinite extension of his existence."

"But he's dead," Lucy said, struggling to understand.

"Not an extension of his corporeal self, of course. The details are not known, unfortunately. Whatever his secret was, it would seem to be lost now. But . . ." Ruth paused and looked searchingly at Lucy. "I do believe there could be some residue, a certain . . . force, still potent, capable of being activated. It seems probable that you activated it. There must have been an ideal conjunction of time, place. . . . I don't know. For some reason you slipped into the dimension that contains his unspent energies. You made contact with them." She was silent, so taken up with her theory she didn't notice that Lucy was silent, too. She turned back, briskly, to renew her study of the wall and paving.

Lucy's voice was feeble in the unstirring golden air. "Do you really believe all that?"

"Indubitably," Ruth said, adding patronizingly, "I think you would be well advised to give some consideration to it. Doesn't it strike you that you're singularly fortunate to be at the nerve center, so to speak, of a magical universe?"

Nothing struck Lucy. She had come to the end of all her resources and there was nothing for her to do except burst out, with scornful northern directness, "Don't talk so bloody daft."

Then she went away.

5

LUCY returned, apologetically, some little time later.

Ruth was sitting on the white garden seat in the yard, thoughtfully smoking a cigarette and gazing at the house.

"I'm sorry," Lucy said. "That was awful of me. I haven't been well," she explained, believing that she hadn't. "And I'm a bit highly strung. Roland shouldn't really leave me alone such a lot, but he had to go off and view a sale. . . . Everything somehow got on top of me. I've made some tea. Will you come in and have some?"

"Sensible girl. A cup of tea is what we both need. Please don't apologize. I understand. This is all very disturbing for you, not quite your kind of thing."

"That's putting it mildly."

They went into the house. In the long, low sitting room, with the sunlight flooding on the shining wooden floor and exquisite rugs, they drank tea from china cups. It was all very gracious and leisurely, Lucy thought, in total contrast to the shrouded, mysterious cellar. "Like sitting on a time bomb," she murmured.

"You mustn't feel like that," her companion said reassuringly. "The vibrations here are excellent: welcoming and benign."

"It's got a nice atmosphere," Lucy agreed cautiously. "I felt it the first time I ever walked in. It seemed to want me, somehow. If I hadn't felt so at home, straight away, I don't think I'd have dared marry Roland the way I did, hardly knowing him, and come all this way down here, away from my friends and family and everything. . . ." She recounted the story of her meeting with Roland, dwelling with naïve pleasure on love at first sight, whirlwind courtship, dreams come true—comforting herself with recollection. After a while, it occurred to her to say, "Oh, but you must know Roland."

"Yes. Not well, I'm afraid. I've lived down in the village all my life. I only moved up to Primrose Cottage a few years ago. I had the privilege of meeting the late Mr. Deane on a few occasions. It was not easy; he kept very much to himself. I did have hopes of a closer association, but . . ."

Lucy leaned forward. The term "closer association" fascinated her; she couldn't quite work out what it meant. She had begun to form the impression that Ruth Drake was a little mad, but mad in the well-mannered, unalarming way that characterized intelligent people.

". . . His physical appearance was striking. He never looked his age, ever. It was remarkable, and certainly gave support to the rumors that he had the secret of some elixir of life. Even when he was very old. He moved slowly, of course, but with such dignity and sense of purpose one could honestly believe that he had command of the elements, that they would yield to him. His gaze was compelling; he looked into one's eyes and one felt—yes, yes—he had looked through layers of civilized response, he had perceived the secret self. . . ." For a moment the large, sensible woman gazed into space, then she collected herself. "He was irresistible to women, naturally."

"Was he?" Lucy breathed, her mind flying to Roland. She searched her mind but couldn't find in any of Roland's physical characteristics a resemblance to his father; there was one family attribute they seemed to share, though. "Roland's like that. The minute I met him, I felt this attraction. I suppose he's inherited it."

Ruth proffered her cup. "May I?"

"Yes, yes," Lucy said, eagerly busy with teapot and milk jug. While she was occupied, her companion said slowly:

"I must be quite frank with you. Your husband does not like me." She met Lucy's startled gaze squarely. "No, don't try to be polite. I'll explain. You may know I'm a writer, like your husband; but I support myself entirely by my writing, I'm a professional. I turn my hand to anything and all is grist to my mill. I move exclusively in the literary world, where I have a wide circle of friends and contacts. I have occasionally, in that milieu, come up against your husband. Although he doesn't mix a great deal, he can afford to pick and choose his company. I can't. That is in no way intended as a criticism."

"Of course not," Lucy said, searching in her mind for something. "I know—I remember. Marleigh. Your name was on the program."

"Yes. I gave a lecture on contemporary magazine fiction."

"I'm afraid I didn't . . ."

"No matter. The thing is, Mrs. Deane, your husband regards me as something of a vulture. I once expressed a wish to write about your father-in-law. I have a genuine respect for him; I'm quite capable of seeing my way to the truth through the welter of highly colored stories that have gathered about his name. His own writings were published privately, in very limited editions. They're practically impossible to obtain—collectors' items, in fact. I've read what I could but there's still a great deal of ground to cover. I wouldn't attempt a serious biography until I had all the facts at my disposal. The ideal would have been to begin in his lifetime; personal contact would have been invaluable. But that was not possible. He was, as I said, inaccessible."

"Did you try?"

"Yes. Your husband discouraged me, actively. He considered me a mere sensation seeker. He still does."

"I'm sorry," Lucy said helplessly. "I don't think there's anything I can do."

"I'm sure there isn't. You mustn't think of it. I would be the last person to cause discord between husband and wife, particularly for my own ends. There is a selfish element in this—one must be realistic, my dear."

She smiled, and Lucy thought what strange contrasts met in

this woman: common sense and battiness, severity and kindness.
"I wish I'd talked to you before," Lucy said, remembering bitterly how she had gone chattering about all over the place to people who were—she could see it now—quite as foolish and second-class as herself. Certainly they had none of this woman's intelligence and integrity.

"I'm away a great deal. In fact, I'm off again next week—lecture tour of America. And I must go now. I'm expecting friends for the weekend and they'll be arriving soon." Regretfully, but with determination, she stood up. "You'll be all right until your husband gets back?"

Lucy nodded. She expected Roland back early in the evening. Her nerves had steadied, the shock had lost its clarity, already there was a tinge of doubt to her recollection of it.

"Would you mind . . ." Ruth Drake was looking through the window at the long sweep of the garden. "Would you mind if I went that way? I can cut through the wood; there's a footbridge across the river. The path brings me out at the side of my cottage."

"Of course." Lucy led her to the dining room and out through the French windows, onto the terrace. The secateurs were lying on the stone wall. Lucy snatched them up, saying eagerly, "Let me cut you some roses. Please." It was the wrong time of day to cut them, and no doubt Ruth had a gardenful; but Lucy wanted to give something, as a way of saying thank you. Ruth, interpreting the impulse correctly, murmured, "How kind. That would be nice. . . ."

They went down to the garden. While Lucy snipped busily away, Ruth admired the clematis and the fountain. Lucy said, "You've been very kind. . . ."

"Please, it was nothing. I do wonder, though, what your husband will make of it. And I wonder if he's had any similar experiences. It is possible. . . . He would keep them to himself, though, I think. Years ago—oh, years ago—we used to call them the secret people."

"Who did?"

"Everyone, really. Everyone round here. It seems such a long time ago. Not ordinary time, you know, but a different age. The magician and his family. Of course, they went about in a normal way, they must have, and yet no one ever really *knew* them, if you understand. The men with whom he was associated in the early nineteen hundreds—in the magical revival, as they called it then—he outlived them all. It was said they abused their bodies—and their minds—in pursuit of the ineffable; drugs and goodness knows what else. Well, if they did, it obviously didn't harm him. He lived to a great age, peacefully, I believe, here in this lovely place with his children."

"Yes." Encouraged to view him as something other than a self-deluded dotard, Lucy thought kindly of the old man for a moment. Then she said, "*What?*"

Ruth glanced at her fob watch. "Goodness, I must go. My guests . . ."

With swift movements Lucy tied the roses together. "Listen—you said *children*. . . ." She trotted after Ruth. "You said children."

"Mm. Mirabelle, of course. The last I heard, she was in America. I wonder if I might contact her while I'm there."

"*Who is Mirabelle?*"

"Your husband's sister. No, wait a minute. It would be half sister, the daughter of old Mr. Deane's first wife. . . ." They halted and faced each other. The roses trembled between them. Soberly, Ruth said, "Mrs. Deane, didn't you know about Mirabelle?"

"No!" Lucy burst out, on a cry of anguish.

"Oh, dear. I seem to have put my foot in it. . . ."

"Wait—" Lucy pleaded.

They were at the end of the garden, where bushes thronged in a green barrier that gave way, here and there, to an open space and the path that fringed the wood. The sound of birdsong was loud and the air filtered on cool currents from the shade of the trees. Lucy looked distractedly back toward the house. She had left all the doors open, but it would be the second time in a matter of hours that she had done so and gone away. It was a terrible day; it kept falling apart around her.

"I'll walk with you a little way. Just tell me about her, quickly."

"In brief, she's an artist, of considerable talent. I should have thought you'd have heard of her. There was considerable publicity when she won the John Moores prize; that's something to do with your part of the world, isn't it?"

"I don't know about art and things like that. I don't understand it."

"I only have rumor to go on for this, so I suppose I shouldn't say it, but one understood the relationship was always . . . stormy. Then, after Mr. Deane's death, there seemed to be a final rupture. They all went their separate ways. . . ."

"*All,*" Lucy repeated, aghast. "How many *were* there, for God's sake?"

Ruth paused and studied Lucy briefly, comprehensively. "It's obvious there was an estrangement and your husband will, understandably, have his own reasons for not wanting to revive old quarrels. As an outsider I'm bound to respect them. As his wife . . . well, you and he must settle things between yourselves, mustn't you?"

Could they ever settle anything, Lucy thought bitterly, when there was so much unsaid, more than this woman could ever guess?

They had reached the river and halted at the footbridge. "I'll go back now," Lucy said. "I hope I haven't made you too late."

"You've had a confusing time. I feel I haven't helped. When I get back from the States you might perhaps call and see me. Depending, of course, on how your husband feels. . . ."

Damn him, Lucy thought. *He doesn't ask me how I feel, having* sisters *sprung on me by strangers.* It was a surprisingly savage reaction for her, and she was ashamed of it. Aloud, she asked, "How long is it, since she was here, at the house?"

"Years, I think. One can't be sure; she always used to come and go. The last time I saw them all together was at Marleigh; but that would be—let me see—nearly five years ago now. Yes, even old Mr. Deane was there, and your husband, and Mirabelle, and —" Ruth was striding across the footbridge, gesturing farewell with her roses. "Chin up. Au revoir. We'll talk again. . . ."

When she was out of sight, and the last suggestion of haste and vigor had disappeared with her, the murmuring peace of the wood closed around Lucy. Low between its banks, the river gathered the colors of the tall grass and densely crowding trees to its surface and like dark green glass, unmoving and never still, looped away into silence.

For a few moments, while her thoughts absorbed her, Lucy stood looking down into the water, where her reflection wavered, tugged by unseen currents, rippling, blurring and re-forming. In a defeated way she said aloud, "Mirabelle . . ." not knowing what to make of her, or of Roland's silence.

She looked around furtively, half afraid that someone might be about, surprising her in the eccentricity of talking to herself in public. People walked there sometimes; she had seen them from the garden. Occasionally she took nervous little strolls herself, always keeping to the path, never going into the trees. All her life she had been accustomed to things that were regulated, manufactured and insensible. She didn't understand the wood, and because she didn't understand it she thought she must be afraid of it. Her mother, learning that something as sinister as a collection of trees lurked at the very border of Lucy's garden, had reacted with self-satisfied outrage, warning Lucy to take care. "Of what?" Lucy asked. But her mother could not be specific. She had no knowledge of such places; she could only mutter that things went on in them, and crept up out of them. . . . Anything was possible.

Certainly, Lucy had never been alone so far into the wood. She thought fussily, *I must hurry*, but her overstrung nerves had slackened and she had paused long enough to realize that she was not in the least afraid. It was amazing. She was not rejecting her fear, or controlling it—it had simply never existed. The ridiculous fancies that had been imposed on her melted away into acceptance. She could walk on slowly, undistracted by her surroundings, and return to her thoughts, to the anxieties that lay beyond and around the peaceful place.

When at last she reached the clearing where the bushes gave way to the garden, she looked back. In the breathing stillness contained by the twisted shapes of the trees, the sun gleamed in dapples of light and shade. The rise and fall of the ground, the irregularity of the trunks, the unexpected thickets, gave an impression of density, of paths going endlessly on, lost and twisting and luring. She felt a moment's regret that she had no time, and other matters claimed her, and she couldn't follow them.

6

A FADED sign at the entrance to the shop claimed expansively to give valuations, buy and sell libraries, search for wants and specialize in the occult. Inside, books were stacked on the floor, seeping out of boxes, tumbling off the counter.

Henry lingered deliberately, aware of scrutiny, whispers, faintly scurrying activity. Then he went to the counter, where there was a small, clear space. After a moment an assistant appeared, standing between the piles of books with the beleaguered air of the last survivor holding the pass. He said dimly, "Yes?"

"I'll see the boss," Henry said.

"He's out."

"He's in," Henry said, his voice clear and quiet and very hard.

The assistant squeaked, "Yes." Occasionally, he argued; never with men like Henry. He lifted the counter flap. "In there," indicating a door shrouded about with shelves of books.

The dealer was a large man, spreading with self-indulgence.

He sat impassively behind his desk, acknowledging his visitor with a grudging nod that combined an invitation to take a seat. He was not a gentleman, but then, neither was Henry. He was, however, on his own ground, which should have given him an advantage. Henry's tall, taut figure deprived him of it in any physical sense, the powerful coherence of bone and muscle being in itself an insulting victory over the flabby man.

"I understand you're an authority, the best. Tell me about this," Henry said, drawing the black book from his pocket.

A greedy gleam showed for an instant in the man's eyes. He handled the book with the negligence of the expert, scarcely glancing at it, passing it back. "It's not worth much."

"I didn't say I wanted to sell it."

"In that case, I'm busy. I charge for information."

"I don't. I'll give you some now, free. On January the sixteenth, in another county where you were in business, you received a suspended sentence of two years for handling stolen goods, namely, nine hundred pounds' worth of books. A fact that can't be said to be common knowledge around here; it wouldn't exactly inspire confidence in your customers. But then, you must be a bit short of it yourself—confidence. You're still on that sentence. You wouldn't like to find yourself serving it, would you?"

"I knew it as soon as I saw you walk in. You buggers never let a man go, do you? You can't touch me. I've done nothing since then."

"Perhaps we can think of something," Henry said, politely unyielding.

"Are you threatening me?"

"Yes."

"You can't do that; you're making a mistake," the man said. Then he stopped, his bluster bouncing mockingly about the close, cluttered room. Men like Henry did not make mistakes, and they both knew it. He sighed and reached once more for the book, asking with genuine curiosity, "Where did you get it?"

"I found it." There was an edge of bitterness to the sudden humor in Henry's voice. "In circumstances where I can honestly claim a right to it. I know it was printed ten years ago by a man who ran a small press, almost single-handed. He died shortly after that was produced and the firm folded up."

"He specialized in this sort of thing. Didn't put out much; most of it rubbish. This," the dealer said reluctantly, "was different. So few copies have ever come to light there are some people who don't even believe it exists. There were said to be twenty altogether; that would be reasonable. I've only seen three. One was in the collection of a man I knew. I offered him a hundred and fifty for it but he wouldn't sell. . . ."

Henry picked up the slender book, momentarily aghast at the extravagant mania of collectors.

"When he died, his family destroyed his library. They thought it was dangerous, blasphemous. It was worth a mint, full of stuff you spend years searching for."

"The second copy of this?"

"Turned up in a load of books from a jumble sale. Marvelous." The dealer shook his head; a certain blankness in his eyes suggested he was dwelling on the treasures slipping out of his grasp in staggering quantities at jumble sales up and down the country.

"Have you kept it?"

"*Kept it?*" The man reacted as if the ethics of his entire trade had been called into question.

"The content has no value, then?" Henry said dryly, wondering if book dealers ever actually read anything.

"I wouldn't know. I don't understand it," the man replied, resolving Henry's doubt. "I put it in auction. It went to a foreigner, a Greek or something. He was over here buying books."

"The third copy?"

"This one."

"I see. Who wrote it?"

"I don't know."

"Come on," Henry said quietly.

"I don't. Nobody does."

The trouble with the transparent look of dedicated liars, Henry thought, was that it became fixed on their faces, even when they were telling the truth. He opened the book and read:

these are the words of Aleph
whose number is one
and one-one-one

Aleph
who has ascended the ten sephiroth
and attained the sacred wisdom
now in the sign of the Pentagram
calls to serve his will

the demons of the air
the spirits of fire
the phantoms of water
the ghosts of the earth. . . .

"So who is Aleph? He must have another name."

"One he was known by, yes. That was his secret name; his power was in it. Anyone who identified him by it could turn his power against him."

"Do you believe that?"

"What I believe I can buy and sell."

"Mm. Why do you speak about him as if he's dead?"

"I think he must be. That was printed ten years ago; there's been nothing since. If there had been, I'd know."

"He could have given it all up, this mumbo-jumbo. He could be living quietly in Southend breeding hamsters. He could be putting out stuff under another name."

"There was a magical revival in the early nineteen hundreds. A man who called himself Aleph was associated with it. If you want to read through all the literature that was churned out then, books, pamphlets, letters, diaries, magazines—if you can get hold of them all—you'll trace a few references to him. It'll take you years and they won't tell you who he was, only what he claimed he could do. It's accepted he was a respected figure then. That suggests an older man, and that was sixty years ago."

"So it is feasible he's dead." Henry picked up the book and looked at it thoughtfully. "The other copies—would he have kept them?"

"It's more than likely. I don't believe any of them should have got into circulation at all; they'd have been meant for believers, initiates, whatever you like to call them. Where did you say you got this?"

"I didn't. Some of the pages are missing. Apart from that, is it the same as the others you've seen?"

"Yes."

"Have a look at it. Make sure."

"I don't need to; I know. But still . . ." The man sat hunched with the air of a miser counting his gold. His fat hands turned the pages slowly. "Yes, it's the same. Nice binding, though."

"Is it? I wouldn't know," Henry said. Then he leaned forward. "Do you mean the others weren't?"

"Bound? Yes, but not like this. It's hand done. This inlaid design is craftsmanship."

"Can you tell who's done it?"

"Fine bindings are all individual, to a degree, some more than others. I could give you one or two possibilities."

While Henry took out his pen, the dealer reluctantly put the book down, saying, "Pity about the missing pages. Have you read it?"

Henry nodded.

"What do you think it's about?"

"Death," Henry said.

7

CROSSING the narrow street to the square, Lucy was almost run down by a bicycle. The bicycle was traveling at high speed but Lucy was paying no attention to anything, so the blame could be fairly divided. Lucy dropped a great deal of her shopping and her handbag, which burst open and scattered its contents over the cobbled street.

Bunty wrenched her bicycle upright, said, "Bleeding hell," without rancor and set about helping to put Lucy to rights.

"It always seems to be *parcels,*" Lucy said on a note of quavering resignation. "Strange women and *parcels.*"

"They're yours," Bunty pointed out. She spoke quickly and clearly in a high voice that would have sounded sharp but for its strangely plaintive quality. All the contradictions of her character were expressed in physical terms: she was very small and moved rapidly, with an exquisitely controlled impatience of everything and everyone; her gestures were flickering and yet fluid; and in her quick little face her eyes dreamed, heavy and dark with melancholy.

"I'm sorry," Lucy mumbled, rebuked by the high, wailing voice and disconcerted by the languid gaze. "I wăsn't paying attention to what I was doing. I've just had a shock; some bad news."

"Tough. Here . . ." Bunty organized her bicycle, Lucy and Lucy's belongings on a seat at the edge of the square. Lucy fumbled for a handkerchief to dab at her eyes. The day was cool and she wore a short blue cotton coat, knee-length white socks and flat-heeled shoes. Her dark hair was held by a blue Alice band. She looked like a child waiting to be collected by a responsible adult. After retrieving a lipstick from a crack between the cobbles, Bunty sat beside her, asking, "What is it?" with great directness and little sympathy.

"I was just speaking to two friends in the Market Hall. They told me . . . they'd just heard. Ruth Drake is dead," Lucy said, taking it for granted that Bunty, whom she had often seen careering about on her bicycle, knew Ruth Drake.

"Poor old beast," Bunty said, in a meditative tone that proved she did. "How?"

"A cerebral hemorrhage. It was dreadfully sudden."

"They generally are."

"Yes. But she was in America, on a lecture tour, not ill or anything. Although it seems she did have high blood pressure but hardly anyone knew. She didn't make a thing about it. It's awful, isn't it?"

"How was it you knew her?"

It didn't occur to Lucy that the question was phrased in an odd, possibly insulting way. She was overawed by Bunty, by her offhand, arrogant manner, her beautiful voice—the tone of which proclaimed her a lady, whatever her startling language might indicate. And her attention was diverted by a furtive recognition of certain comparisons: they were about the same age, of similar coloring and build, but . . . Lucy sighed, mentally resolving to diet, be more positive, and stop wearing beige. "What? I don't suppose I could really say I *knew* her. Something nasty happened to me once and I met her then by a sort of accident; she was very kind and sensible and understanding."

"She was a tough cookie. But then, who isn't?"

"I'm not," Lucy said indignantly.

"No, you're not." The sooty-lashed eyes slid to her, amused, slid away.

"Well, I'm not very bright, so maybe I'm not much of a judge of character. But she seemed to me to be really nice. Very eccentric, of course . . ."

"What was the something nasty?"

Lucy fiddled with her handkerchief. "I prefer not to speak about it. I've got over it now."

"Good. If I were you, I'd carry some smelling salts. You appear to live in a state of permanent crisis." Bunty looked at her watch. "I wonder if I had any breakfast."

Lucy stared at her. "Don't you *know?*"

"I can't remember. I don't think I could have—I'm terribly hungry. I must go. You're all right now, aren't you?"

"I'm still very upset," Lucy said, reluctant to release this vital creature and go back home to an empty house. Roland was off once more buying books, or selling them; she was not quite sure and had no interest.

"Still, you've got your car and you're all right to drive. It's not far."

"No," Lucy agreed, assuming the remark to be the result of observation. Lucy noticed everything and everyone, smiling eagerly at people she was accustomed to seeing about in the hope that they would smile back. "Could you lunch with me? Would you? It would be nice to talk to someone who knew Ruth. We could go to The Feathers."

"Thanks all the same, but I'm terribly busy," Bunty said, rejecting the invitation with careless grace. "I must go." She got up, flung herself at her bicycle and an instant later, without a backward glance, was pedaling away, dodging in and out of the traffic and ringing her bell.

The track was wide and curving, the trees stood back from it, courteous as dancers, and here and there the boughs of the tallest met overhead. The man who walked the track moved with the conspicuous nonchalance of someone very large trying to look invisible. A few houses lay clustered ahead, to his right, but he didn't need to pass through them. And from them only the most determined observer would have caught sight of him, and then perhaps presumed he was following the track around and down behind the houses, to the footbridge over the river and into the wood.

At the point where the track curved and dipped, Bunty's house stood, its small garden crowding around it, giving it a secret air. Her doors were always open and the man knew this. As he slipped into the side door, his stealthiness left him and a gloomy determination took its place.

He went through to the back of the house, to her workshop. She said, "Oh, Cedric, not again. Go away." But he wouldn't. He stayed too long, knocked things over and got in her way. Her sharpness had no effect on him; he knew the other Bunty, the tender, sensual woman, and he clung to his knowledge of her. But she had claimed back from him that part of her nature. His references to past intimacies embarrassed her to the point where she wished there had been none at all to refer to. "Honest to God, Cedric, don't you think it's crass to keep talking about my *body?* After all, it *is* mine."

"It was mine once," he reminded her, dolefully importunate.

"No, it wasn't. I only lent it."

"You said I was the best—"

"Oh, don't. Oh, Christ, the vanity of the male. There are certain things women always say at certain moments. They don't have to be true." The plaintive note in her voice was pronounced. "Go back to your wife. How did you manage to get away from her, anyway, on a Saturday?"

"It's Friday."

"Is it? Oh, good, I've got another day to finish these." She picked up a pile of books in varying stages of disrepair and lurched across to her workbench with them.

The big man watched her in silence for a while. He had never been even faintly interested in her work, although he had pretended to be, to please her. Their time together had been limited, and mostly spent in bed. Now that she had discarded him as a lover, he had time to regard her in relation to her work. That her quick little hands could work so deftly and with such loving patience should have been a wonder to him, but he scarcely noticed. He had always resented the least thing that took her attention away from him.

"I haven't seen you since last week. Last market day. You were sitting in the square talking to little Lucy Deane. I was going to come over but you suddenly jumped up and went off. I wondered if you'd noticed me."

"I never notice anything," Bunty said truthfully.

"I don't want to bring any trouble on you. I couldn't bear that."

"Bugger off then, or you will," Bunty said. "I don't know how we ever got away with it. Your wife's got eyes like a buzzard. She talks to everyone and makes you account for every minute. If you carry on like this, calling on me, ringing me up, somebody, *somebody's* going to find out and—"

"That was why you finished with me, wasn't it?" he interrupted, looking at her solemnly. "If it had all blown up . . . you couldn't face the scandal."

"I couldn't face the inconvenience. The emotional wear and tear, all for nothing."

"You liberated women, you don't pull your punches. Was I nothing?"

"Stop being *pathetic*," Bunty said, exasperated. She had sorted through the books and was making notes on slips of paper of the work she would do on each one. The window behind her looked over the narrow back garden, where greenery climbed high stone walls and tumbled about haphazard steps that went down to the river. The day had the vaporous, spreading light of sun behind cloud and was so still not a leaf moved in the garden. "What I meant was that there's nothing for anyone to make a fuss about now. Your visits here are boringly proper but I can't see you or anyone convincing your wife of that. She's a total bitch but I don't want to hurt her just for the hell of it. She needs you—"

"She hates me."

"Yes. But she still needs you. To trample on. And you let

yourself be trampled, you even expect it. You expected it from me, and that's degrading, for both of us. You might have a marriage that's completely lacking in dignity, but you're not going to have an affair as well. Not with me anyway."

"You've got somebody else, haven't you?"

Bunty said, "Eeeek," quietly, desperately, and returned to her work.

"I'm not blaming you. You're free to choose whomever you want. . . ."

"I *haven't*, though."

"I don't believe that."

"I don't care."

"You need a man in your life. You're so passionate."

"I can control myself, you know. And I wish I had where you were concerned."

"I know you think I'm a drag because I can't leave you alone, but—"

The doorbell rang, cutting off his words with its sudden, imperious trill. He leaped up, knocking over a pile of strawboard for the second time. "I never locked the door."

"I should bloody well hope not. This is my house; you can't go locking doors on a whim. Go out the way you came in. They're ringing at the front, whoever it is. . . ."

He was trying to organize himself, spreading panic in wasteful movements. "Go into your living room and look through the curtains."

"Certainly *not*. This isn't some ghastly adulterous suburb. Now, I'm going to answer the door. I don't care what you do."

He sped clumsily before her, down the two steps from her workshop to the oddly shaped hall, wrenching open a door and stepping into the long, whitewashed porch that was built along the side of the house. "I'll wait here till you open the front door. . . ."

"Oh, God, it's not *worth* it. Never again. Never, never a married man again," Bunty muttered.

"Keep them talking, whoever it is, and they won't see me go."

But Henry, standing at the half-open front door and listening to the hurried conversation, didn't need to watch Cedric go. He had seen him arrive.

He stood on the threshold, his tall figure emphatic against the background glimmer of the overcast day. He dressed too well, with a dandified attention to detail and neatness. His dark hair, fashionably long, was carefully brushed. He was attractive and polite and his smile restrained what was resolute and possibly dangerous in him.

Already disconcerted to discover the door half open, Bunty said, when he had introduced himself, "Don't I know you?"

"No." He smiled again, shook his head. He had a book tucked under his arm. "I bought this at the secondhand bookshop in the village. It's in rather a bad state. They told me you could rebind it for me."

"Of course." She invited him in and led him to the kitchen, where she made tea.

He said, "Thank you, I'm ready for that. I've been wandering about, admiring the houses and their gardens. It's delightful, tucked away at the end of the road, almost falling into the river. Not the kind of place where anyone can say they dropped in because they happened to be passing. One has to come deliberately."

Her absorbed, melancholy eyes studied him before she said, "Quite." She poured the tea, without ceremony or apology, into china mugs. "Come into my workshop." She led the way, saying, "You're a stranger. Are you staying here?"

"Yes. At The Feathers."

"Business or pleasure? Mind—two steps up."

In the shadowed corner of the hall, he had almost tripped on the step. She moved so lightly, so swiftly, he had the impression she could go blindfold about the odd little house without touching anything. And in the workshop she was so much at home among the papers and boards and leathers, the tools and equipment, everything seemed merely an extension of herself.

He looked around. "What a fascinating place. Do you work here all by yourself?"

"Mm. Do sit down, if you can find somewhere. Let me see your book." He handed it to her. "Local antiquities. Nice. You're interested?"

"Very. I'm doing something I've always intended to do—taking a couple of weeks off from business cares and just looking around. Churches, buildings, old hill forts, that sort of thing. I thought I'd use the village as a base; it's central to strike out anywhere. And quiet. I'd like to get some stuff together for a book. This seems the ideal place to do it."

"Good. You must be quite an expert."

"Oh, no, not at all. An enthusiastic amateur with a longing to see my name in print. An amazing number of people start with very little more than that. An interest in the subject is vital, of course, plus application, painstaking research, a basic knowledge of grammar and enough nerve to believe that someone, somewhere, wants to read what you've written."

"A thoroughly practical approach; you're bound to succeed. More so than people with a message who agonize."

She laughed, and he laughed, too. "Oh, I met enough of those at Marleigh as well."

"Marleigh . . . I've got the most terrible memory; is that where I've met you?"

He studied her with open, inoffensive admiration: her silky brown hair cut raggedly around her small face, her enormous dark eyes, the rosy brown blush on her cheekbones where the sun had caught her. "No. I never forget anyone, and I couldn't have forgotten you."

"So . . . you're lurking in Nine Maidens looking at monuments. All by yourself."

"Does it sound sinister?"

"No. Lots of people do it, but if there is a type, you don't look it."

"I know, thank God. They're generally to be found striding

about examining hill figures: magnifying glasses and baggy shorts and legs like knotted string. It must be something about the subject that attracts earnest nuts. Principally, I'm interested in the religious aspect and the adaptation of paganism to Christianity. I believe there's a lot of evidence round here."

She looked at him consideringly. "Try the village church. You never know what you might find."

He thought a smile touched the corners of her mouth, the merest wicked suggestion of a smile, but her back was to the window and a play of light on her face could have deceived him. He went to stand beside her at the workbench, where he could see her clearly. "I only arrived yesterday, so I haven't seen it properly, not yet."

"You must. Parts of it are very early Norman."

He could think of no response less likely to commit him to error than a simple "Ah . . ." It was true he was interested in the subject, but his knowledge had always been superficial and he had only recently begun to study it in more depth. Fortunately, there were so many different theories covering any one of its aspects, he was confident he could cover up any mistakes he might make by claiming he was putting forward a new interpretation. The people he had spoken to had always obligingly divided into two groups: those who knew nothing at all, and those who knew so much they preferred to talk, not listen.

Bunty was different, something in her attitude shifted his confidence toward doubt; but he made conversation, asking her opinion on areas and landmarks of interest. They drank their tea and smoked cigarettes and talked in an almost companionable way, and all the time the suspicion that she was laughing at him lurked just beneath the surface of conscious thought. She moved about as she spoke, not restlessly but in her elusive, gliding way. He tried to watch her, to keep her face clearly within his vision; but always, it seemed, when she encountered shadows she encountered that wicked hint of a smile. He would find himself leaning toward her, uneasily saying, "I beg your pardon?" and she would turn toward the light and repeat what she had said, her face innocent with polite interest.

At last, he grew exasperated. He was not accustomed to being at a disadvantage, and it was worse still not to be sure that perhaps he was not at a disadvantage at all, that it was his imagination, or the strange light, playing tricks.

He stood up. "I must go. How long will it take you to do that book?"

"I can't start on it just yet. Will the end of the week be all right? Yes? Cloth or leather?"

"What do you think?"

"Oh, cloth. I've got a nice blue. Shall I show you?"

"No, I'll leave it to you. I hear you have excellent taste."

"Good." She did not ask who had told him that. Self-possessed, she looked at him, her impatience stilled into waiting.

"Will you have dinner with me? Tomorrow."

"Thank you. Yes."

"I'll pick you up at eight."

She drew a sheet of paper toward her and wrote on it in a surprisingly large, decisive hand: *8 p.m.* "What day is it tomorrow?"

"Saturday," he said, and watched her write the day.

"I forget practically everything," she said, by way of explanation and, perhaps, apology.

He took the paper, borrowed her pen and wrote his name in even larger letters. "That's so you won't forget me. I'd hate to walk in here and have you calling me Bill, or Roger."

A faintly guilty look on her face indicated that this had happened, then she smiled. "I won't forget who you are."

He turned to go. She sat on the stool at her workbench, making no move to show him out. "The doors are always open, for going out and coming in." She reached for the books she had begun to work on earlier, selected one and turned all her attention to it, as if he were no longer there.

He waited for a moment and then went back to stand beside

her. "There's something else." He placed himself where he could read every change in her expression; but she said, "Yes?" without looking up.

From his inside pocket he drew the small black book and put it on the bench in front of her. She made no move to touch it, there was no change of tone in her high, plaintive voice, and yet indefinably her attitude took on the tension of surprise. "What's that?"

"I picked it up," he said easily. When she said nothing, he asked, "Don't you know it?"

"Should I?"

"It's one of your bindings, isn't it?"

She put her elbow on the bench and rested her chin in her hand in a thoughtful pose. Her head was tilted to one side, revealing her small face, attentive, considering. "Don't think so. I've done —oh, I couldn't count how many. I don't remember them all. Why do you ask?"

"It's something of a curiosity. I'd like to identify it."

He stood beside her, his senses working so keenly he detected the faintest physical tremor, scarcely more than a vibration. He slid the book along the bench a little nearer to her and in an instant, with her quicksilver grace, she had slipped off the stool, out of reach. "Well, it's all blindingly interesting," she said. "However, I must get on with some work. Will you excuse me while I get some water to damp this. . . ." She waved a piece of leather at him and went out, not closing the door but pulling it so that it stood slightly ajar.

She had been too quick for him; just how quick he didn't at first realize. He made use of her absence to go to her boxes and racks of finishing tools to examine them to see if any one design matched the emblem on the cover of the black book.

One by one he had tracked down the names on the list the fat book dealer had given him. It had taken time, and he was too experienced to let lies or evasions slip past him. Even so, he had uncovered nothing. When he had exhausted all the possibilities, he tried an outside chance and consulted the Designer Bookbinders. They had suggested Bunty and supplied her address. The information had brought him to Nine Maidens, to stand in her workshop to review in his mind her disturbing charm and even more disturbing elusive air, her unmistakable reaction to the black book—

Suddenly, he was aware of two things. First, he was staring at a large bowl of clean water on which a sponge floated, ready for use; second, or simultaneously, a sound registered on the corner of his attention. He whirled around, snatching up the book and pushing it into his pocket as he ran to the door, taking the two steps in one stride.

The emptiness of the hall was the utter emptiness of someone precipitantly gone. He ran into the kitchen. The window looked out on the side of the house and an angled view showed him where the track dipped to the footbridge and her flying form, vivid between the trees, as she bicycled wildly into the wood.

He found the side door, wrenched it open and—not knowing he had to turn left and then right to get out of the porch—almost crashed into the whitewashed wall. The uneven paving was hazardous; tubs and pots of flowers encumbered him—deliberately, it seemed. He knocked something over and cursed. He had never been clumsy; he was furious with himself.

By the time he was over the footbridge, she had vanished. Leading into the wood were three paths of flattened earth, too dry and rock-hard to show any impression of recent tracks. He stood still, straining to catch some sound, however faint, that would indicate which direction she was traveling. There were faint stirrings in the trees, birdsong, the cooing of pigeons, the liquid whisper of the river; nothing to suggest an impulsive woman hurtling along on a bicycle.

There was nothing for it but to guess. He chose the path that led straight ahead. It was slightly wider than the other two, affording her the chance to be more quickly out of earshot. As he set off, he cursed her for a devious, bewildering bitch. And a liar.

She had lied to him about the book. She recognized it, and her recognition of it impelled her to do this extraordinary thing—leave her house and everything it contained to the mercy of a complete stranger while she went chasing off. Where? And why?

He strode along, trying to hear some sound above the noise of his own footsteps. The path branched to the left; a scattering of dust on the grass at its edge prompted him to follow it. The path narrowed, twisted, split again; he had the absurd feeling that the wood was deliberately closing in on him. Eventually, when there was yet another choice of direction to make, he halted and got his breath.

There was no sun by which he could orientate himself. He knew the wood was not large; unless he walked around in circles he could not walk for very long before touching its boundary. He had a moment of doubt: *was* he walking around in circles? Something had to account for the sudden, overwhelming impression of vastness; the stab of uneasiness—so acute it might almost have been panic—that he was imprisoned in a glimmering green world where unseen, inimical presences reduced him to helplessness and mocked his confusion.

He squared his shoulders. He was a city man, he didn't understand trees, the infinitesimal movements of growing things. The unfamiliarity of everything around him had effected a temporary dislocation of his senses, that was all. He looked around. This was not his element, but he was not going to let it defeat him.

8

THERE was no warning of her approach, no sound, no hint of movement.

One minute Lucy was alone in the dining room, contending

with one of her aggressive flower arrangements—and the next minute Bunty was there, standing at the open French window in an attitude of beautiful repose, as if she had been there a considerable time and just chosen that moment to materialize.

"You—" Lucy gaped. Bunty moved, flickering into the room before Lucy's astonished gaze. "What do you want?"

"Roland," Bunty said.

Lucy's surprise quickened to indignation. "What *for?* What do you mean, just turning up here? I didn't even know you *knew* him."

As she walked across to the door that opened onto the hall, Bunty spared her a glance; and not even Lucy, ready to meet anyone more than halfway when it came to common courtesy, could read any apology in it. "You can't— Here, wait a minute —" She had a slight start and the impetus of shock. She reached the door first, slammed it and leaned against it. "Where do you think you're going?"

"To see Roland."

"Well, you can't. You can just jolly well explain yourself."

They faced each other; they were exactly the same height, but Bunty's fragile, vivid body expressed an arrogance Lucy could never hope to combat. She said, "Shift, you silly woman."

"How *dare* you—" Lucy cried, the wildest notions multiplying in her head. "What gives you the right to come in here and insult me and demand to see my husband? I don't even know you—I've only spoken to you once. Last week. You knocked me over with your bike and you wouldn't come to lunch with me."

"Oh, Jesus," Bunty breathed.

From the hall Roland called, "Lucy, what's the matter?" The door heaved forward as he tried to open it. Lucy heaved back against it.

"You're not coming in until this woman has explained herself."

"*What* woman?" he called, pushing at the door again.

Then there was a moment of total inactivity, a silence into

which Bunty spoke Roland's name, once, in her clear, unmistakable voice.

The door heaved again and Lucy lurched forward. There was no scrambling collision. Bunty seemed merely to melt away, to be standing in a waiting pose as Lucy collected herself ungracefully, somewhere about the middle of the room, and Roland entered.

"What do you want?" he said.

"I must speak to you."

"Who *is* she?" Lucy shrilled.

"What about?" Roland asked, ignoring her.

"I wouldn't come if it wasn't important."

They spoke and regarded each other in a manner in which there was a reluctant intimacy, an acceptance of needs and priorities. Lucy, humiliated beyond the state where she cared about humiliating herself further, burst out, "I know, I know now. It's her, isn't it? That's what's wrong; all the time it's been her. . . ."

"Lucy, control yourself," Roland said, not coldly but impersonally, as if he were speaking to a child who had threatened to be sick.

"No, I won't. I'm fed up controlling myself. I've been controlling myself since I married you and I can't stand it another minute. . . ."

In a voice in which impatience was tinged with contempt, Bunty asked Roland if he couldn't stop Lucy from making a scene.

"You—you tart. You posh tart," Lucy cried. She heard the ugly stridence of her voice and knew she sounded just like her mother in one of her rages. Not even the shame of that could stop her. "I know about you. Everyone knows about you. You have affairs with other women's husbands."

"Not in the plural, I don't," Bunty said.

"Vera Legge's husband. Everyone's been talking about you and Cedric. Everyone knows, except"—her voice faltered—"Vera. She doesn't know."

"With you around, it won't take long," Bunty said, adding in a faintly puzzled voice, "Do they really? In that case, I think I've just made a mistake about something."

Lucy's fury slackened. She was increasingly aware of behaving disgracefully and increasingly sorry for herself; she considered she had every justification. "Roland, why did you marry me if you're in love with this woman?"

"Don't be silly. She's my cousin."

Lucy gasped and sat down on an armchair.

Bunty said thoughtfully to Roland, "A man, who's just been to see me . . ."

"Who?"

"Yes, who? That's the point. Tall, dark, tough sort of dude, like a cowboy spruced up for his night out. Oh, sod. I thought he might be one of those inquiry agents, checking up on me for Vera Legge. She wouldn't need one, would she? She could just ask her friends and save the expense."

"Does it matter?"

"Not about that. Not in the least. The other bit's important." Bunty glanced toward Lucy, who had found her voice again.

"*Your cousin.* I've been married to you all this time, and she's been living down there by the river, and you never even *told* me. How many more damn cousins and sisters and God knows what have you got? Hiding. You haven't told me the truth about anything. Why did you marry me if you didn't want to tell me things? Why did you marry me if you didn't want *me?* . . ." Her voice dragged out into a wail.

He went to her and surprisingly took her hand for a moment. "I do want you. I married you because I love you," he said. There was a hard sort of hostility in him which she sensed was not directed at her. If it was meant for this self-possessed intruder, it was contained within some intricate convention, like the rules of a game only they could understand.

"You don't care about me," she complained. "You don't care about anything except your secrets and your quarrels. I wouldn't have known about Mirabelle if Ruth Drake hadn't told me. *She* was kind to me, *she* believed I had that awful experience in the cellar. . . ."

Roland leaned toward her. "I didn't say I didn't believe you, Lucy."

"No—but you told me it didn't matter, you told me to forget about it."

"What?" Bunty asked. "What was it?"

She spoke to Roland, but Lucy answered. It was *her* story and she was going to tell it. She launched herself on a description, exaggerating, growing incoherent. Deep down, some part of herself was immensely gratified that Bunty was listening attentively, without the hint of a smile. Her satisfaction collapsed when she paused to sob and Bunty observed, "Oh, God, she's getting hysterical again."

"I'm *not*," Lucy yelled. "It's my nerves. I can't help it. Ever since then I don't know what's real and what isn't. That awful dream when I saw him coming out of the wood . . . Roland said it was a dream, he said it was the sleeping pills, but it *felt* real. . . ."

"Tell me," Bunty said.

Lucy jumped. Absorbed in herself, she had not noticed that they had changed places, that Bunty was standing over her now. Roland had gone to the table where she had been working at her flower arrangement. He was idly picking up flowers and leaves and putting them down. Once he glanced at Bunty. And at some moment Lucy had lost in her noise and weeping a tension as faint and tremulous as a spider's web had gathered about the room.

"What dream? Who came out of the wood?"

"He did. That . . . magician. I thought I was asleep—no, I didn't. I thought I was awake but I must have been asleep. Something disturbed me and I got out of bed and went to the window, and he was there, in that clearing between the end of the garden and the wood. The moon . . . it was almost like daylight."

And he had stepped out of the silver-margined blackness of the trees, moving without haste in his terrible dignity, the substance of his form lost in the long, stirring folds of the cloak, the moon white in the eye holes of the hood that obscured his head. . . .

"I put my hands over my face. I couldn't speak, I couldn't move. I don't know how long I went on standing there. When I looked again—there was nothing. I think I fainted. . . . I woke up, or came round, or something, and Roland was lifting me up from the floor."

Bunty looked at Roland, who said, "I think she dreamed, and got out of bed in her sleep and went to the window."

"Yes. That would be it," Bunty said.

"Would it?" Lucy asked, with pathetic appeal. All she wanted was reassurance. "I'd been taking sleeping pills, because I'd been so upset about that other business, and I'm not used to them. It was on my mind, you see. I suppose you're used to the idea, like Roland. Well, I'm not. I think it's a lot to expect me just to accept it—I mean, most of the time I can't even believe it. . . ."

Bunty had moved away to stand across the table from Roland; they regarded each other wordlessly. *They don't need words. . . .* The understanding moved and was lost in Lucy, leaving nothing but a petulant awareness that they were excluding her. She began to complain. "I think you should make allowances for me. I think you've been mean to me, Roland. You could have told me she was your cousin. I could have made friends with her. I haven't got any friends. . . ."

"She's at it again," Bunty murmured.

"What can I do?" Roland said, as if to himself.

"Slug her. No, perhaps not. It's better if she gets it all over at once, like a fall of soot. Lucy, be a good soul and go and make us all some tea."

"So you can *talk*," Lucy said. "So you can talk about *me*, and make clever jokes, and be superior. I don't have to put up with this, you know." It occurred to her that the classic tactic of a woman in her position was the threat to return home to mother. The mere thought of it sobered her. She stood up, fortified by a defiance that almost passed for dignity. "I shall make tea. Just to show you I don't care."

Henry found the boundary of the wood and doggedly followed it: the trees on his left hand, on his right the tall hedges and fences of gardens. He couldn't know why she had gone, but it was important he discover where. If necessary, he would keep on walking until nightfall.

Through gaps in one hedge he saw a field where glossy ponies cropped at the lush summer grass. Then the path spread to a clearing, and instead of a hedge to mark the end of a garden there was shrubbery, clusters of bushes that looked impenetrable. But when he approached he saw there were openings, a miniature labyrinth of softly trodden paths that led into the garden.

He went a little way into the bushes. A glint of blue and silver caught his eye. He moved toward it and saw it was a bicycle, flung down where the bushes ended. He looked at it thoughtfully. It was not concealed, it was just . . . abandoned. His gaze traveled up the garden, up the different levels of steps and rockery and ribbed lawn. She could scarcely ride it up there, or drag it with her; she would simply leave it and walk up to the house.

He chose a position where he couldn't be seen from either the path or the house, and waited. He recorded the details of everything he could see, very methodically, in his mind. After a while she appeared on the wisteria-hung terrace with a man. They walked down the steps and moved about the garden, talking.

On the terrace a woman lingered, her aimlessness, her exclusion eloquent even across that distance. She watched them, too, and he watched her watching them: shredding her handkerchief between her hands, smoothing her hair with distracted movements, scuffing her sandals on the terrace steps. Then going sadly, clumsily away.

9

"I HEARD about you from headquarters, sir," Sergeant Collins said. "Anything I can do?"

"Let's look at the map," Henry said. "I'm going to describe a house to you."

The sergeant looked, and listened. "That would be young Mr. Deane's. Low white house, next to the field with the horses. Yes."

Henry began to describe Bunty, which was not necessary. The sergeant smiled. "Miss Meacham, yes. You mustn't mind too much what she does. She's a bit of an odd one."

"That's throwing roses at it," Henry said. He was weary and dusty and thirsty. When he looked at the map he was amazed at the ground he had covered. "I haven't done so much walking since I was on the beat, and then it was only the natives that were hostile. That bloody wood."

"It's supposed to be enchanted, sir. Just a local superstition."

"I believe it," Henry said feelingly.

"Shall I get the missus to make us a nice cup of tea?"

"Thank you. You've only been in the area two years, I know, sergeant, but have you ever seen this woman during that time around here?"

The sergeant studied the photograph Henry handed him, shaking his head. "No, sir. Sorry."

"No . . . Now, what about Miss Meacham? and the Deanes?"

"It's not something that's talked about much, but you get to know these things in time. It's said she's the illegitimate daughter of old Mr. Deane. He died about four years back; strange old cove, by all accounts. There was another daughter. She went to live abroad some time ago; I've never seen her. Then the son, Roland. Like his father, antiquarian book dealer, bit of a literary man. Lives very quietly. He married recently."

"A small, plump, brown-haired woman?"

"That's her. Pleasant little thing, always ready with a smile and a chat."

"Is she? Good," Henry said. "Why was the old man strange?"

"Well . . ." The sergeant's bland expression solidified. He was about to get the improbable over first, in a few words. "It's said he was a magician."

Without any apparent reaction, Henry stared back. "Go on."

Making a furtive trip into the hall while she prepared the tea, Lucy heard scraps of conversation. Roland said, "You know the force that was there. It was a long time ago, but it was almost tangible. It hasn't dissipated." . . . "Yes, all right. But why didn't you come and tell me instead of arsing about in your half-baked way. You know what we agreed." Roland said something about managing things on his own and Bunty interrupted: "You can't, you silly prune, you never could. Look at that time at Marleigh when you came back here for a couple of days. . . ."

Roland answered in a muffled way, perhaps because he had moved across the room. Whatever he said, Bunty burst out in answer: "All right. But letting that book out of your hands was the stupidest thing." . . . "It was what Father wanted." . . . "And now it's turned up again. It's got to be that one—we could account for all the others." . . . "Could we? I'm trying to think. . . ." For a while they murmured speculatively, their voices rising gradually in disagreement, Roland saying accusingly, "You know your trouble? Your trouble has always been your arrogance, your shattering bloody excessive arrogance." . . . "And yours has always been that you have the soul of a provincial grocer. However, I'm not holding that against you, I never did, so shut up. We've got to think. There are two things involved here; we've got to sort them out."

There was some movement in the room; their voices became indistinct. Lucy shrank back and then advanced again, catching stray words: "connection" . . . "fifth element" . . . "Mirabelle." Their voices mingled in some scornful contest which Bunty won; she could speak more quickly, more bitingly: "I admit nothing that threatens me." . . . "You don't know." . . . "No, and I don't want to know. Remember that. But why now? Why now, all of a sudden?" Roland said, "I thought it was all over. I thought it had finished."

The whistling kettle screeched. Lucy started and fled into the kitchen. She couldn't begin to guess what they were talking about. She meant to make them tell her, instead of treating her like a fool. Whatever it was, she thought, dashing milk into the jug, she was on Roland's side, against everybody; even that horrible dead old wizard.

When she carried the tray into the dining room, it was obvious they had declared a truce for her benefit. There was no satisfaction for her in it, only an awareness of her exclusion: fighting, which separated other people, seemed merely to have brought them closer together. With some determination she said, "I think you should tell me what's going on, Roland."

He stirred sugar into his tea, looking at her almost absently. "Nothing to bother you, Lucy. It's . . . er . . . family business."

"*I'm* your family."

"True," Bunty murmured, in a manner obviously calculated to irritate Roland, not encourage Lucy.

Lucy said doggedly, "I don't think you're very polite. I don't think it's polite of you to turn up, just like this. *Or* not to tell me, when I was talking to you on market day, that we're related by marriage."

"His fault. Blame him, not me," Bunty said. Her careless gesture toward Roland grew still, took on deliberation. She narrowed her eyes, very slowly shaped her hand to resemble a gun, and sighted it on Roland. To Lucy's amazement, Roland raised his hands, saying, "Don't shoot," in a strangled voice. Bunty drawled, "You've taken your last ride, Montana," and went "*Pow*" softly, jerking her hand. Roland toppled forward, burlesquing a spectacular death.

"Stop it," Lucy said faintly, staring at them. Whatever was troubling them, they had simply put it aside. Their tension had disappeared. Forgetting her, their age, their hostility, they had immersed themselves in some charade that had beguiled their lost, long ago childhood. "You're mad," Lucy shouted, and they looked toward her, their hidden laughter fading.

Without a trace of self-consciousness, Roland dusted himself and took a cigarette. Bunty said, "Garsp . . ." piteously, and he grinned and tossed one to her. She turned to Lucy, saying severely, "No, we're not. Every family has its funny little ways. I bet yours has."

"My family don't hide about, pretending not to be. My family don't have peculiar people who—who do things in cellars."

Bunty said, "While we're on the subject . . ." and looked at Roland.

"Lucy, would you like to go and visit your mother for a little while?" Roland said.

Lucy shouted, "*No!*" and met no objection at all. Their lack of reaction disconcerted her. She had to justify herself, claim some loyalty from Roland. "Why do you want to board me out like a dog? *Why* don't you want me here? You know I can't go and visit my mother yet; we haven't been married long enough. She'd guess something was wrong. And my nerves are in such a state. And you *know* what she's like."

"What is she like?" Bunty asked.

Roland said she was indescribable and Bunty gave her sharp laugh. "Isn't that typical of you, to get landed with a music-hall mother-in-law."

"Oh, she's not *funny*," Roland said.

Bunty said, "Ah," drank her tea and looked into the cup with a faint air of surprise. "I've *had* tea, haven't I? Oh, yes, with that feller."

"You'll have made a big impression. Just leaving him there."

"Doesn't matter. He'll go away eventually. The thing is to get—to get it off him."

"How?"

"I'll do it," Bunty said.

"*What?*" Lucy asked. When they didn't answer, she burst out, "This is like being in a fog. Why are you so unkind to me? Why won't you *tell* me anything?"

Roland said, "We will—but, Lucy, you mustn't go talking about this to your friends."

"I don't bother with my friends much at the moment. In fact, I don't bother with them at all, only you haven't noticed," Lucy complained, hating the way Roland said "We." She sat up, in an attentive attitude, clasping her hands. To her surprise, it was Bunty and not Roland who began to speak.

"Some years ago, just before he died, my father—"

"If you're Roland's cousin, he must be your uncle."

"No, he *mustn't.* Does it matter? *Roland's* father . . . carried out a certain ceremony. It was . . . um . . . a sort of experiment."

"I thought he was always doing it," Lucy said.

"Do you want to listen? Or would you rather interrupt?"

"I'm sorry," Lucy said meekly.

"He was. But this was something different. It was something he had to do before he died—*because* he was going to die. It needed skill, and stamina, and courage. When you focus these things in cabalistic magic, when you implement them, there are bound to be . . . vibrations, pressures: the greater the effort and arcane knowledge behind them, the greater the pressure. Naturally. This was enormous, stupendous, because it was his last act, and his greatest daring: an attempt to perpetuate himself."

Something stirred in Lucy's mind, something she couldn't quite grasp. She looked toward Roland, wondering why he was letting Bunty tell her. Reading the bewilderment on her face, Roland said, "My father existed in two worlds: the one we see about us, and the invisible one. The invisible one consists of abstracts: will, thought, intelligence. These things are projected into this world to everyone, in some degree. Certain people, exceptional people like my father, can perceive their source—sometimes it's called astral light—and can convert this light into energy."

Bunty spoke; her voice had the merest, fleeting irony. "He said his body was just a shell, it had passed through several incarnations. By means of the astral light he generated a greater build-up of power each time. This impelled him to a more perfect state through successive incarnations."

Roland said softly to Bunty, "And you doubt your own doubt! Disdainful woman. He achieved physical perfection; when we were small he was like a god. What did time do to him?"

Bunty lifted her head and tilted it proudly, considering. "All right. He was splendid. But I never said he wasn't."

Lucy interrupted excitedly; she had recalled what it was that had been teasing her memory. "No. He looked into your eyes and saw your soul. He was ageless—Ruth Drake told me. And she said that about him living forever. Or something."

A spasm of irritation crossed Roland's face, to be replaced by a guarded look. "You never told me that bit, Lucy. Did she say anything to you of the sort of thing we've just told you—about the ceremony of the fifth element?"

"The what? Oh, you mean this experiment before he died? No. Do people know about it?"

"No, and you mustn't tell them," Roland said shortly.

"Well, I won't, I won't. I'd have a terrible job anyway; how can you explain something you don't understand?"

Bunty gave a rather wicked smile and said, "Dear Lucy . . . such a comfort. I'm beginning to see why you married her, Roland. Now, you've got it straight, haven't you? There were some vibrations left after the ceremony, they were dormant, for some reason they became active at the exact time you were in the cellar."

"Yes," Lucy said. The extraordinary business was unlikely to remain in her mind in any coherent form, her obstacle to understanding being not doubt but incomprehension. They spoke in such a matter-of-fact way, they accepted the outrageous without the flicker of an eye—their familiarity with the unknown gave them an authority she found totally convincing. She would believe anything they told her, these strange people. Because the awful truth, the only truth she could at that moment grasp, was that Roland was strange now. He had undergone yet another transformation and this time she didn't have to study him, and puzzle and wonder. She had only to look at Bunty, and back again to Roland, to see the same challenging, careless pride, the physical poise, the maddening, elusive air. How could she hold her marriage together when she never knew, from one week to the next, what sort of man she was married to?

10

ONCE again, the door was half open. Henry stood with rain on his dark hair, in an attitude too elegantly studied to suggest anything except retaliation.

Bunty was waiting, her long green dress as vivid as washed leaves, her hands clasped a little demurely. "I remembered," she said. "Bill. Or is it John?"

"Try Cedric."

"Oh, no. You couldn't be a Cedric. Even if you tried."

"You haven't just shoved him out of the back door again, have you?"

"Certainly not. If you even suspected that might happen, you wouldn't have come. It would be an affront to your masculine vanity."

"It would be monotonous, too."

She laughed, tilting her small head. The light moved over her curly brown hair. She had brushed it, he saw, brushed it and brushed it until it shone, ragged and soft. He went up to her, close to the breathing sweetness of her scent. Her makeup was flawless; she had taken a lot of trouble for him.

She said, "Do you know what I thought? I thought you were one of those sordid people who collect evidence for a divorce. Which would serve me right for getting involved in a sordid situation. There was a certain dreadful amusement in it. Especially when I thought you were just making up a story to account for being here. So I had a game with you, I teased you. I'm sorry. Will you forgive me and start again?"

"Of course." With so much pride, so much self-possession, perhaps she thought he wouldn't notice that the mistake she had made was not the one for which she offered her graceful apology. He took her small, strong hand and touched the palm with his lips, a gesture of faintly mocking intimacy. Her fingers tensed briefly and her dreaming eyes took on a sudden guarded glitter.

"Oh . . . and then I left you. How eccentric of me. I'd remembered something, you see."

"An urgent appointment, perhaps."

"Yes. I hope you didn't wait long. When I came back you'd gone. I told you I had a shocking memory. It makes me do things like that."

"Not tonight, I hope."

She laughed her quick, plaintive laugh. "No. Not tonight."

Sometime in the evening the rain stopped, and when he drove her home the drenched green of the trees and the colors of the small gardens had faded into an exquisite glinting blue dusk.

Her house was untidy, with good, modest furniture that had worn serenely over many years in its service of giving comfort. She had insisted they return there for coffee, although it was early. The evening had been delightful. He had a suspicion that she was allowing herself to be charmed by him as deliberately as he was charming her. They had talked lightly of many things, she had flirted a little with him; and when they danced she had not talked at all but simply let him hold her in his arms. He was so conscious of the fragility of her body, its delicate, provocative movements, he had an unnerving moment when he feared the least miscalculation by which his strength could crush her.

in her chaotic kitchen she made coffee, pouring it into the china mugs that seemed to serve every purpose—he noticed that some had brushes standing in them, or curious gluey substances.

"You wanted me to show you my workshop. Come along," she said, leading him in. There were leaves of books strung along on lines.

"Like wash," Henry said.

"That's what I've done. Washed them. They're dry now. You don't mind if I see to them? It won't take me long."

She took down the sheets and set about refolding them. She worked so swiftly the flickering movement of her hands on the white paper made him blink. With only the angle-poise lamp over the bench switched on, the room had a shadowy denseness, and it was warm, strange scents of glue and chemicals mingling in a faint dampness.

He was aware of the beginnings of a headache and deliberately focused his attention on what she was telling him, what some of the equipment was for, how she used it. He examined a book lying on the bench, admiring the intricate gold tooling. "I see," he said, "the tools don't have special shapes. They're all sizes, straight, curved—you build up a design."

"That's right. Some of them are special, marvelous little things —animals and birds and flowers. . . ."

He thought how soft her voice was, how the silence spread away round it; even the paper made no sound as her hands moved in their pale rhythm, backward and forward, backward and forward. . . . Pain stabbed behind his eyes. He could not understand it and tried to ignore it, turning his head slowly and looking about. "That huge press—it's medieval."

"Isn't it? Some of the equipment, the processes—they haven't changed for hundreds of years."

"But it's enormous, and you're so tiny."

"Oh, I'm very strong, though. I have to be." She was beside him, leaning against him so gently he scarcely felt the pressure of her body, which was remarkable because her body was what he had come for; as well. And she knew that, too. He cursed the headache, willing it to go away, and smiling down at her felt the pain drawing into her dark, dreaming eyes.

"Let's go into the sitting room." Her hand found his, tugging gently. He stumbled on the two steps and she said, "Are you all right?"

He mumbled something. As he sank onto the enormous sofa, she said, "The air—it's close in there, and the smell of chemicals affects people sometimes. I'm used to it."

"I'm sorry. My head . . ." he muttered, drawing her small, pliant body close and searching for her eyes, where there was no pain.

She said, "Ohhh . . ." like a sigh, and touched his forehead with her moth-cool hands.

His half-formed desire wavered and his hold on her loosened. It wasn't necessary to hold anyone so insubstantial; she was so close to him he was almost absorbed in her—or she was absorbed in him. Hazily, he attempted some distinction. The effort was enormous, like the leaden-limbed motion of dreams. And it didn't matter, nothing really mattered. He thought he would tell her this and there was a blissful moment when even his voice had ceased to matter. Some instinct moved him sluggishly to grasp at understanding; he put words together slowly, laboriously, in his head: *I . . . wonder . . . what's . . . happening?* and uncovered a distant warning, faint and unfocused.

Then he began to struggle, despairingly, out of habit, knowing that all the strength of all his life was being weakened by a sliding, shifting power. His will, entangled, began to slacken, and the rage that would save him dissolved into torpor. She floated unreachably before him, lost in shadows. And he died, or went to sleep; and dreamed.

It was a humiliating dream. Robbed of balance and impetus, he strove in a phantasmagoric world. His stifled fury, grasping only the sense of the lost coherence of his limbs, urged him into a directionless lurching through changes of light and shade and air; and of the unbelievable things that became believable to him he accepted nothing, and strove again, and in a bursting, defiant effort, blundered back into reality.

He was leaning half-collapsed against a gate on a narrow, moonlit road; his smarting hands and dampness on his clothes told him how the evil blackthorn hedges had clutched at him on his way. There was the sound of an owl, a screech folding weirdly into the time and the place and the silence where the dream lay. But he was safe now. His head cleared rapidly and he functioned once again with decision. It took him no more than a moment to pick up his bearings, to calculate how far behind him the tree-guarded track opened onto the road. The town lay not too far ahead and he began to stride toward it.

He was not running away; he knew nothing about running away. He knew when blind force paid off and when caution was necessary. He had learned the hard way, and it had made him hard. Now he faced a situation totally new. Even in his furious amazement he acknowledged his ignorance, because to deny it would render him powerless. Silently, grimly, he promised, *I'll fight you. . . .*

He had made a start. He did not know how she had induced the dreadful, ecstatic enchantment of the dream state any more than he knew what resources inside himself had reacted against it. He only knew that he had countered it at some primitive level used by something inside himself that would not give way. And that—he smiled as he went swiftly along—would at least make her wary of him.

The small town went to sleep early, and it was past the hour when the pubs closed. There was still activity in the rambling, oak-beamed hotel: some people leaving, guests sitting in quiet conversation over late drinks. Henry paused long enough to pick up his key and tell the receptionist, "Let me know if anyone telephones."

His room was tucked away down an uneven, creaking corridor. It was chintzy and comfortable, sharing with the rest of the hotel the slightly crazy charm of very old buildings. Practically any key would fit the simple, worn lock. Henry drew the curtains before switching on the light and went straight to the place where he had concealed the black book.

It was gone, as he had expected, but he did a great deal of swearing because it made him feel better. A trace of her sweet scent lingered on the air. The room had been searched carefully, but in an amateur way. But then, he thought, she was an amateur; it would never have occurred to her to look in his pockets, where she could have found the photograph and his identity card. And there on the dressing table, to puzzle him, to tease him, or simply to show her disdain—his car keys.

He began to undress, interrupted by the telephone. The receptionist said, "There was a lady on the line for you, but I'm sorry, she seems to have rung off, Mr. Beaumont."

"Thank you." Checking up on him. He had not stayed where she had put him; she was just careful enough to find out where he was.

When he was ready for bed, he switched off the light, drew back the curtains and sat in the deep embrasure of the window, smoking a cigarette and thinking.

Whatever it was she had done—hypnosis? probably; and something else, something he could not explain that briefly touched a chill to his spine—she had not expected him to fight back. At least, when she discovered he could, she hadn't underestimated him. She knew he would follow her, limiting her time, making it impossible for her to return to her house. So she had left his car down in the square, taken the book and gone away with it. . . . Where?

Beyond his window the town shrugged into sleep, leaving the night to its secret whisperings and stirrings. This was her territory; it was useless to go out and look for her. His strength lay in what she believed to be his weakness. She would calculate his skepticism, his city-nurtured ignorance, his maleness, and never think him capable of an act of imaginative daring—of seeing her landscape as she saw it, and according her her place in it.

11

IN a shady corner of the garden, Lucy struggled to thin out a dementedly overgrown philadelphus. Enveloped in its heavy scent, with white petals shaking down on her, she worked on. She was trying not to think about Bunty, who, since her abrupt arrival, seemed almost permanently in residence. Occasionally she disappeared, perhaps to her own house, and then reappeared in her soundless and always surprising way, giving Lucy a faint suspicion that she had exchanged one hiding place for another.

Lucy didn't ask. She had practically given up asking questions; even if there were answers, she could scarcely understand them. She longed for an ally and in an overwrought moment even considered sending for her mother, dismissing the thought instantly. Being unable to do anything positive, she took as little action as possible about most things. Bunty pottered about, spending time with Roland in his study talking books, or being surprisingly domestic in her offhand way, washing up and vacuuming carpets. She fitted into the house as if she had never been away. She knew every corner, where everything was. She kept to herself any criticism she might have of the changes Lucy had made. Once or twice she observed casually, "That's nice. New. Nice," and Lucy, not expecting approval of any kind, didn't know how to respond and was ungracious.

The hot evening closed in. Lucy had been in the garden for hours. She was dirty and hungry and presumed that Bunty was at that moment preparing the dinner. Someone had to, and *she* wouldn't. . . .

But she was hungry and wondered how long she would have to wait. Unable to help herself, she craned around the bush to look toward the house. The French windows were open and Bunty could be glimpsed just beyond them, moving about at the dining table.

They'll call me, Lucy thought. And then, stricken, *Supposing they don't? Supposing they just sit down and eat?* The personal insult took second place to her horror of going without food. She was always preparing to go on a diet and always stoking up for the day that she did, which accounted for her plumpness. She sighed and looked around the garden in the indecisive moment before she made up her mind. Then she turned and tidily sought out her clippers and secateurs and, turning again, looking out from the transparent green shelter of the shrubs, she caught her breath and stared.

A woman stood in the garden, just beyond the fountain. A tall, slender woman with glinting pale hair that fell softly to her shoulders. She wore a long dress that had the blurred and floating colors of sweet peas; the faintest motion of the material suggested that she had that instant paused. She reached her hand forward in a languorous greeting gesture and smiled toward the house.

Without even being aware that she had turned her head, Lucy followed the direction of the smile and saw Bunty, standing on the terrace with her arms outstretched, answering the greeting. Her long dress seemed to spin about her in a flash of jade as she darted down the garden, slowing her step to balance her pleasure in the tilt of her head and, again, the lovely outward sweep of her arms. "Mirabelle . . ."

They kissed, consideringly, and spoke to each other in voices hushed and laughing. Lucy couldn't hear what they said; she didn't expect to hear. The scene revealed itself with a dreamlike grace before her eyes. She was not aware that Roland had approached, simply that he was there, his presence absorbed effortlessly, without sound, without a ripple of air. He kissed Mirabelle, and when Lucy saw him standing close to her with his arms around her tall, slender body, she felt a pang that wrenched her back to reality.

Sounds swelled around her: their voices, the early-evening clamor of the birds, the splash of the fountain. Feeling at once conspicuous and superfluous, she began a hesitant approach. When their smiling and unsurprised faces turned toward her, she knew that all the time they had been aware of her. Aware, disregarding, waiting for her to find her own moment, her own words. Her smile was stuck so resolutely to her face it was almost painful. "May I join the charmed circle?"

Mirabelle said, "Hello, Lucy."

Lucy wiped her sticky hands on her gardening dress in preparation for a handshake, a kiss. Obviously none was required, as no one introduced her to Mirabelle. Left once more to find her own way, with all the polite props of convention removed, she had only her smile for support. Shored up by it, she made murmurings: "How nice . . . what a surprise . . . are you staying?"

Bunty said, "Of course. Din-din's in half an hour. Let's have a drink," and then they were all moving toward the house. Aghast, Lucy made a mental comparison of their appearance with her own. She muttered, "I must change," and sprinted forward. If they laughed or made reference to her, she didn't care. On the terrace, she glanced back. They were moving slowly through the glitter of the evening, talking, gesturing, their bodies turning toward and away as if they were treading the steps of a stately, elaborate dance to music only they could hear.

The scent of stocks drifted in through open windows as the garden blurred into dusk. At the long table, Bunty and Roland and Mirabelle, guarded by candles, sat in elegant attitudes. Lucy studied them, seeking to trace the family likeness feature by feature, losing it in the distinction each face claimed. Mirabelle's eyes were extraordinary, of so pale a blue they seemed without surface until Lucy looked into them, then she felt herself drawn down into lightlessness, depth on depth, falling forever.

She was afraid of Mirabelle, yet her fear had been taken from her and distilled into admiration. In some other place, some other dimension where all normal responses operated, she would find it again and be amazed. But in a time that was a suspension of time, to be with her and Bunty and Roland and share the simple act of eating a meal became a disconcerting privilege. They talked idly, of matters of no importance. When their conversation was too elliptical for her to follow, when they made jokes she didn't understand, she let her incomprehension show plainly on her face; it was all she had to offer and someone might—and occasionally did—enlighten her. Often she made no pretense of listening; then her silence became part of a deeper silence where all senses were expanded: colors were richer, scents more exotic, the invisible currents of the night trembled, carrying the reverberant harmony of their voices to a stillness beyond sound.

"Do you know what a scrying glass is?" Mirabelle spoke, addressing Lucy.

Lucy shook her head, defenselessly aware that she was about to find out. Mirabelle turned to pass a wordless message to Bunty, who got up and went away.

"It's a crystal ball," Roland said, speaking to Lucy but looking at Mirabelle, who returned his oblique irony with her smile.

"For fortunetelling," Lucy said brightly.

"Something like that," Roland murmured. "Bunty's quite good with one."

"It gives a girl something to do in the long winter evenings," Mirabelle finished solemnly.

Lucy strained briefly between their barricaded glances. "Is this serious?"

Mirabelle said, "Oh, yes. You see, we want to find out, if we can, why you felt the influence of my father so strongly."

Lucy said to Roland, "Did you want to find out? You never said. You never bothered."

"I was waiting. We must all be here; it's necessary."

"Why?"

Mirabelle answered, "We were very close to him; our awareness of him was refined through years of contact. Being together, the three of us, naturally there's an accumulation of our telepathic ability. We have a greater chance of receiving what's channeled through you, and of interpreting it."

Lucy said awkwardly, "I thought—I had the impression that Bunty doesn't—didn't believe in him."

"Not exactly that. Not everything he claimed. She has certain reservations," Mirabelle said, in a tone that implied she shared them.

"You haven't," Lucy said to Roland.

"No."

She had a distant apprehension of conflict, the complexities of which were beyond her. She concentrated on the immediate fact that she was about to be used as some kind of filter. How? She murmured uneasily that it was all a bit odd, knowing that her definition of the word meant nothing to them. "I don't see how you can do it. . . ."

"We have gifts of our own," Mirabelle said calmly, turning her strange eyes on Lucy.

"Yes," Lucy said, without argument; held by that lightless gaze, she could believe anything. "But . . . you don't want me to go in the cellar, do you?"

"No. Here will do. . . ."

Together, Roland and Mirabelle rose, drawing Lucy between them in a drifting way to a small table in the center of the room. With a start, Lucy saw that Bunty was already seated there. She had returned without sound sometime during their conversation, choosing as her place the rim of darkness where candlelight wavered into shadow, waiting silently, her pale hands folded against the muted brilliance of her dress. On the table before her lay a wooden box, the lid of which, divided into two halves, had opened out flat. In the central portion a beautiful rock crystal lay in a velvet-lined hollow. Lucy looked closely, straining in the uncertain light to make out the design of leaves carved on the box.

"What shall I do?" she asked.

"Just sit opposite me. Look into the glass. Pretend you're in the cellar again."

Bunty's voice was unchanged, sharp and plaintive, and Lucy felt let down. If she had to remember something unpleasant, shouldn't she be helped toward it by a more soothing tone—told to relax, perhaps, or breathe deeply? "Shall I empty my mind?" she ventured.

"Why? What have you got in it?" Bunty said, casually sarcastic. "Oh, all right, do what you like, only sit still and shut up."

Lucy glared indignantly at the glass. She was tempted to get up and go away, but she knew if she did they would blame failure on her and despise her for not being equal to the occasion. Random thoughts occurred to her, unassociated with the event she was supposed to recall. Her mind remained stubbornly fixed on the present, monitoring only the immediate: the very faint concerted breathing, the whispering movement of Bunty's dress, the pinpoint of light mirrored on the surface of the glass. Curious to know the source of the light, she looked up, saying, "It's no good. I can't do a thing just because you tell me to."

"Yes, you can," Bunty said.

Mirabelle and Roland stood close together, and Mirabelle's hand lay on Bunty's shoulder. Grouped as if for a portrait, they waited, their bodies distinct and yet merging together, linked arm by arm, hand by hand, in a sensuous, rhythmic stillness. Their skin tones had a glimmering, softly changing luster, and half-glimpsed smiles faded in the shadow of each face. On Mirabelle's hand a ring

Yes you can Bunty said

glinted, as distant as an eye of light at the end of a tunnel, its brilliance beckoning

Yes Bunty said

the shapely hand disintegrating. The light expanded, pulsing gently, and Lucy was drawn into its beautiful deception, its beautiful forgetting.

12

MRS. Cartwright, severely welcoming against the backdrop of Benares brass and stags' horns, said, "You are a man of great persistence, Inspector."

"All policemen have to be," Henry said.

"With you it's something more than the line of duty. Please forgive a personal observation, but it seems such an unlikely combination: the fleeting Smith—and you."

"I suppose so. I appreciate your kindness in arranging for me to see Mr. Thwaite here."

"Not at all. When you telephoned and said you wished to speak to me again, also that you intended getting in touch with him while you were here in Marleigh, it seemed to me that it was simply more convenient. After all, we have been lifelong friends, and see each other frequently."

They spoke across the chill grandeur of the drawing room, Bartholomew Thwaite having retired to the privacy of something called "Reginald's smoking room" to read the photostat copy of *The Fifth Element.*

"I've read Mr. Thwaite's book on the history of magic," Henry said.

"A definitive work," Mrs. Cartwright murmured.

"Yes. You'll know, of course, that he refers to Aleph in it, taking care to point out that he had to rely on hearsay, rumor, secondhand reports, and his sources were by no means reliable. He even expresses a doubt that Aleph existed at all."

"True." Mrs. Cartwright nodded. "Which does make it incredible, I agree, that a few years ago Bartie and the man he did not believe existed were here together, in Marleigh. And that I myself . . ."

"Tell me," Henry said.

"Yes." For a moment Mrs. Cartwright sat in composed silence, ordering some sequence of events before she presented them. "This family, the Deanes. I never realized they had any relevance to your inquiries or I would have mentioned them on your first visit, Inspector; I don't gossip for the sake of hearing my own voice. In a curious way, I have nothing to tell you, and yet what I know of them I shall never forget. That year they were here, I used to see them—this was before anyone identified them to me. Once at a Bach recital in the cathedral, once driving in their car, a Mercedes, I think, once walking on the city walls at dusk—a romantic setting, I grant. But they had a curious quality that somehow suggested they would always gravitate toward the romantic, the unusual; a quality I can only describe as eye-catching, although I can't define it. It had nothing to do with the way they dressed—here in Marleigh at Festival time we are accustomed to people of eccentric, not to say outrageous, appearance. They dressed extremely well; not conventionally, it's true, but in a manner entirely, and elegantly, their own. They were physically graceful, you see, and aloof, and their unity invested them with such a purpose they seemed set on a course from which no one could deflect them. One had the extraordinary notion—and I am not a fanciful woman, Inspector—that their destination was not so much a place as a state of being."

She paused and looked at him sternly, as if daring him to argue. He said, "There are other people I've spoken to today who've described them in similar terms. If you're being fanciful, Mrs.

Cartwright, you've got company. Go on."

"The third time I saw them I was accompanied by a friend, to whom I said, 'I feel I ought to *know* those people.' He said I was bound to, and pointed out Mirabelle Deane, the artist, whose name I do know and whose work I admire; the younger woman, Miss Meacham, who had some exquisite work on show in an exhibition of modern bindings; the young man, whose name I was not familiar with but who I understood to be a writer; and the old man. 'There,' my friend said—I should explain he is irreverent, as all the young are—'there stands your actual twentieth-century magician. How does that grab you, Cartwheel, baby?' The amazing thing was that it didn't. I mean, somehow I wasn't even surprised."

Henry was. He had a mental image that almost sent him sprawling. How dare a woman as rigid as a monument have a young male friend who called her Cartwheel, baby? And how dare she report his conversation verbatim, without the twitch of a smile?

But Mrs. Cartwright, devoted to accuracy, was too immersed in her narrative to consider its stray effects on Henry.

"I learned they had rented a house by the West Gate. I sent round a note addressed to Miss Deane, introducing myself and mentioning the name of mutual friends. I commented on her work, which I do sincerely admire, and said I would be pleased to welcome her and her family to one of my soirees. The date I specified was a rainy day—of course—but in the evening the rain stopped and the air was very pleasant and several people went into the garden. It got to be quite late and I thought they would not come. I went out into the garden and—extraordinary—there they were. I'll never understand how I missed them—I'm most punctilious about greeting guests; Reginald was, too. . . . However. Come with me, I'll show you."

In the sunny afternoon, a breeze frisked through the garden, tossing stray leaves in a rather improper fashion at the awful white statues. Midway down the garden there was a formal layout of roses and some seats, one curved and facing the house. "They were there, sitting, standing—disposed, one might say—about that curved seat. . . . As if they had been there all the time."

Henry nodded toward the wall. "The back door."

"Very probably, although no one had actually seen them come in, and they weren't at all the sort of people who would go in anywhere by the back door. Naturally, Reginald and I made them welcome, got them drinks, sat and chatted. I was fascinated to be at close quarters with them. They were charming, an odd sort of charm, difficult to pin down . . . not small talk. And one sensed a tension; nothing impolite, you understand, that would embarrass one; more a—a concentration of force, something gravitational, holding them together. Occasionally people came up and chatted and drifted away. The old man was so striking, very frail and yet compelling. He and Reginald talked about Oriental mysticism, and I must admit my mind wandered. You see, I'd been extremely worried about my sister. She had been ill and I hadn't heard from her—I didn't mention the matter, of course. To my astonishment, Mr. Deane suddenly looked at me and said, 'You will hear from your sister tomorrow, at noon, Mrs. Cartwright.' "

"Did you?"

"Yes. Exactly at noon. I'm not going to ask you if you can account for that, Inspector, because you can't. And I can't, and that's that."

"Mm. Thought transference."

"It had to be, there's no other explanation— Ah."

With shuffling sounds, Bartholomew Thwaite emerged from the house behind them, blinking in the sunlight. He was an incredibly elongated man with the look of a benign stork and an absorption of manner from which he surfaced occasionally with faint surprise, as if the world had overtaken him and proved even madder than he suspected. "Bartie," Mrs. Cartwright said, addressing him with an archaic familiarity Henry found strangely touching, "I'm telling the Inspector about the evening the Deanes were here. Let us walk to the rose arbor."

"Capital. Interesting, most interesting," Bartie murmured.

They went down the garden. Bartie manipulated himself into a sitting position, Mrs. Cartwright sat to his left, gesturing to Henry to take the curved seat, where he faced them at a slight angle.

"I'll tell you this because it is relevant," she said to Henry. "The ground at your feet is soft, you'll notice, and it was that night, too, because it had been raining. The old man had a stick. With the point of it he drew something on the ground. I leaned forward to look because it was still light enough to see. It was a strange sort of design, which I'm afraid I can't describe. At the time he and Reginald were talking of correspondences. . . ."

Mrs. Cartwright paused and looked toward Bartie, who had folded himself in such an attitude that he appeared to have gone to sleep on one leg. Nevertheless, he took up his cue at once.

"Ah, yes. The classification of the features of the universe by linking them each to each. No doubt you are familiar with the system of correspondences, Inspector?"

"I couldn't say that. It's much too extensive for me to grasp. But broadly, I understand that when a magician embarks on a certain operation, he does so on the day and hour allotted to the planet he has chosen and the planet has *its* own association with a certain color, a certain precious stone, a certain metal, and so on. So if the correspondences are wrong, the magic is wrong, even dangerous. In other words, if there's an *odd* link, the chain won't hold."

"Excellent. Most succinct," Bartie murmured. He leaned toward Mrs. Cartwright. "Specifically, my dear?"

"The words of power. And the elements."

"Indeed. The words of power, articulated by Eliphas Levi, are: to know, to dare, to will, to keep silence. As part of a particular ritual, the magus will call the elements to his control by integrating them—your links in the chain, Inspector—thus: to know corresponds to air, to dare is water, to will is fire, to keep silence is earth."

Mrs. Cartwright said, "Yes. Now, when it came to enumerating them, each of the family named them in turn. The magus spoke the words of power and they answered, very softly, quite naturally, as if they were holding a conversation. It had an extraordinary antiphonal effect, really very beautiful, and gave one the feeling that they were saying something of a significance beyond the grasp of any outsider. It was almost as if they were personifying the elements they claimed—which was merely fancy on my part, but if you had seen them and heard them . . . The magus said 'to know' and 'to dare' and Mirabelle and Roland answered 'air' and 'water'; he said, 'To will corresponds to fire. To keep silence . . .' and Bunty answered, '. . . corresponds to earth.' They stopped speaking, and somehow one listened—as if for a strain of music dying away. Then the magus said, 'When these elements are gathered together into the control of the words of power, there arises from them a fifth element, and this is "to go." Its correspondence is spirit—the spirit emerging from perfect equilibrium to journey through time and space to unlock the secret of the universe. . . .' "

Certainly they had telepathic and hypnotic gifts, Henry thought, but what was so vital was their belief in themselves. Sustained by illusion, myth and ritual, they had the ability to utilize their surroundings: they did not react against anything; they absorbed. They would take that moist lowering evening and make it all their own. The distant murmur of voices, a laugh fading somewhere in the garden, the sweet scents the rain had sharpened, the bizarre statues, reared in ponderous immobility —these were scenic effects to which, by their faith in their own fantasies, they brought a touch of magic that worked on the imagination of the onlooker.

Mrs. Cartwright said, "It was while the magus was speaking I became aware that they were all looking straight ahead. Their faces had shades of expression so fine—amusement, irony, tenderness. I turned and looked . . . there." She gestured to where some shallow steps marked a change in the level of the garden. "Smith was standing there. Just standing. In her rather crazy clothes and, for once, nothing impetuous about her at all. She began to walk towards us—not *me*, of course—towards *them*. She came and stood between Reginald and me, as if we didn't exist, and waited very quietly until the magus had finished speaking. I said one was aware of a tension; one was also aware, inescapably, that it had increased. No, I didn't imagine it. There was something as positive as a movement in the air, an invisible thread, tightening—around them, around her—drawing her in to them, holding her fast. The magus said, 'Tell me your name,' and she answered, 'Smith.' 'Smith,' he repeated; then, with his stick, he drew the letter *S* into the design on the earth—"

Henry stood up, thrust his hands in his pockets and made one or two impatient steps about the arrangement of seats. "It's ridiculous. The only time I can get people to speak about her—articulate, intelligent people—they become utterly subjective, they speak in terms of playacting, drama. . . ." The few bitter words worked out his exasperation; he sat down again suddenly.

"We are not trained to keep a cool head, to assess and observe and deal only with fact," Mrs. Cartwright said.

Henry said, "Ouch."

"Quite so," Mrs. Cartwright said, a trace of humor in her reproof. She took from the pocket of her sensible dress a surprisingly bashed-looking packet of cigarettes and offered one to Henry.

"The design . . . it's on the photostat of the title page," Henry said to Bartie. "Will you show it to Mrs. Cartwright?"

She scarcely needed to study it. "Yes, it's the same. I'm sure of it. And what is that, Inspector?"

"A letter. From Smith. Her last letter." Henry smoothed it gently. It was worn at the creases and had a frail, pathetic look. He held it forward. Mrs. Cartwright and Bartie might be almost suffocated by curiosity, but they were still too well bred to read anything not intended for their eyes. They looked only where he indicated. "Why, yes," Mrs. Cartwright said. "That is it again, with the letter *S* added. Isn't that so, Bartie?"

"Indeed . . ." Bartie murmured. He appeared to wish to say nothing more and withdrew into absorption, his beaky face thoughtful.

But Henry leaned forward, forcing the old man's attention. "This emblem, this design—it's a talisman."

"Yes. A symbolic representation of the desire of the magus."

"And that"—Henry indicated *The Fifth Element*—"is his desire written out for a few, a privileged few, to read. And you understand it."

"There are the missing pages. . . ."

"Do they make a great deal of difference?"

"For the performance of the ceremony, yes. It can only be conducted by a highly skilled practitioner, a man with considerable arcane knowledge and advanced powers of concentration. Its success depends on its ritual exactitude and it is not possible to fill in the lacunae by guesswork."

Henry's voice was suddenly hard. "I'm not talking about performing it. I'm talking about understanding it."

"Yes, I know you are, Inspector," Bartie said, and sighed.

Mrs. Cartwright looked from the sad face of her friend to the controlled determination on Henry's. She stood up. "I shall make some tea, I think. Please come into the house when you're ready."

Henry sat stiffly on the uncomfortable sofa and drank tea.

Mrs. Cartwright, proffering cucumber sandwiches, said, "As I see it, Inspector, you have returned to Marleigh because you are now convinced that what you need to know has its beginnings here. Armed with irrefutable facts, you will be able to proceed. No one will ever be able to say, 'You were wrong, you misinterpreted, you omitted.' No one will ever be able to turn you back. Such facts as there are I have contributed to in some measure; namely, Smith was here, the Deanes were here. They met, and certainly became associated in some way because I saw her with them on one occasion afterwards. Now, Bartie's contribution is conjecture—on the basis of this." She indicated the copy of *The*

Fifth Element. "Incidentally, may one ask what became of the original?"

"It was in some luggage that Smith left in a house where she'd stayed. I took possession of it, and it was stolen from me. Luckily, I'd already taken the precaution of having that copy made."

"Very wise," Bartie said. "Might you not discover who stole it and get it back?"

"I know who stole it. A member of the Deane family. It could be destroyed now. I'm sure all the others are."

"How unfortunate," Bartie said, with academic regret. "A member of the family? Are you certain?"

"Absolutely." Henry turned to Mrs. Cartwright. "Briefly, that book explains a ceremony of high magic that was specifically designed to prolong the life of the magus. A ceremony he intended to perform in his old age when he felt death was drawing near. Accompanying him through all the phases of it would be a . . . disciple, someone who was the flesh-and-blood embodiment of the spirit 'to go'; whom he refers to sometimes simply as 'the spirit,' sometimes 'the giver,' or 'the favored one.' The ritual can't proceed without this person; an essential is their absolute willingness to participate and to receive the spirit of the magus—because that, according to Mr. Thwaite's reading of it, is what would occur: a transference, an interchange."

"Indeed," Bartie said. "One must, of course, always keep in mind the factor of the missing pages. They appear to be concerned with the responses of the disciple. . . ."

"Could you conjecture?"

"I would hesitate, particularly on a cursory reading. Closer study might yield something." Bartie's beaky face moved doubtfully from side to side.

"I'll leave it with you, then. If I take it back to Nine Maidens, I've no doubt it'll disappear," Henry said, thinking of the impulsive, light-fingered Bunty. He wrote out the address of his hotel and passed it to the old man. "If you come up with anything, will you get in touch with me, please? I expect to be there for at least another week, possibly a fortnight."

Mrs. Cartwright said, "You're thinking, Inspector, that Smith took the part of the disciple. Would she lend herself to such . . . fantasies?"

Suddenly, Henry felt a drift of anguish, but he said, "Of course," abruptly. He could not afford the luxury of premonition, or despair; he could not afford anguish.

Mrs. Cartwright looked at the way he sat, with his head down and his expression hard. Coolly, she echoed, "Of course."

Henry said to Bartie, "What about the other three being involved in the ceremony?"

"I doubt it. The instructions are somewhat ambiguous regarding the initial stages—the preparation—but I doubt it. An act of transcendental magic cannot be performed by anyone in a normal state: that is to say, the magus consecrates himself to his task by purification, fasting, meditation and prayer. In this case, the disciple is required to accompany him, step by step, through the preliminaries. The union of the two—the oneness, the wholeness—is stressed again and again, pointing to the exclusion of any other party or parties. And during the invocation of certain discarnate entities by the magus—a hazardous business—the presence of any outsider would interfere drastically, even nullify the entire operation."

"But they would know—the others. They would know what was happening—you said earlier that the rites would last days, not hours."

"You are assuming it took place?"

"I'm assuming nothing. I'm covering all the possibilities."

Bartie studied him for a moment before saying, "I don't see how they could fail to know. Look at it this way, Inspector: they were part of his magic, they had been steeped in it since childhood, they existed in his time, in the world he made for them. They may or may not have believed in him, but their conflicts would be internal, and consuming. . . ."

"Was he mad?" Henry asked brutally.

"There are degrees . . ." Bartie murmured.

"There are absolutes. Life and death. You can't bugger about with those. I beg your pardon, Mrs. Cartwright."

Mrs. Cartwright, busy sorting through some magazines, reacted with the merest nod. Looking at her, Henry thought, *Under all that starch she's solid granite. It would take a charge of dynamite to shake her.* She said, "As a theory it's interesting. He could have been . . . unreliable, but his family, who were always with him, would know how to deal with that. It would account for their aloofness, the tension one sensed. . . ."

"How I regret," Bartie mourned, in his faded voice, "not being present the night they were here, my dear. A migraine kept me away. . . . And oddly, I never saw them about the town."

There was nothing odd about it to Henry. Bartie would probably not see anything or anyone unless he was picked up, shaken and pointed in the right direction.

"Here it is," Mrs. Cartwright said, producing a color supplement. "A special art edition, with photographs of paintings from various exhibitions. I remembered it while I was making tea and thought I would get it out to show you. There's a painting of Mirabelle Deane's that might interest you."

Henry took the magazine and studied the photograph. "My God, it's weird!"

Robed and hooded, the magus stood in the center of the picture. Chasms of shadow opened before his feet and a strange light flickered about him, distorting his body and outstretched arms. His figure emerged from a background of trees whose slender columns blended and separated in sensuous movement, giving an impression of density, of depth shifting upon depth. Curious creatures glided through the trees, engrossed in fantastic posturings, defined only by their wicked, glancing smiles; and where the light caught them, it illuminated them in the very moment of their vanishing into the green and silver darkness. The mysterious, manic world belonged to them, to the rhythm of the trees, to the merciless eye of the moon that glittered overhead.

The sumptuous robes of the magus were merely wrappings upon the broken body of a puppet, the folds at the point of collapsing inward, the eye slits in the hood already empty.

Bartie, leaning over Henry's shoulder, murmured, "How interesting. That picture is laughing at something—somebody. A silent shriek of laughter; one can see it. My goodness, one would hate to *hear* it. . . . So interesting, though: the curious figures, the sense of meaning beneath meaning. It puts me in mind of the tarot."

"It puts me in mind of something else," Henry said. "The view from the house. That's the clearing there, and the wood. That bloody wood."

13

THE receptionist, ringing through to Henry's room, said, "There's a Mrs. Deane to see you, Mr. Beaumont. In the lounge."

"Thank you," Henry said, and thought for a moment. Why Mrs. Deane?

At the entrance to the lounge he paused. The only person there was a small, brown-haired woman with a trusting face. She stood at one of the low, round, polished tables clumsily sorting out her shopping, to the peril of a bowl of anemones. Henry reached the table in time to save the flowers. "Good morning."

She said, "What?" a little blankly, fighting with a string bag. "Oh, I should have put all this in the car. I'm Lucy Deane. Mrs. Lucy Deane."

He saw how ill at ease she was, how her nervousness made her awkward. He said, "How nice to meet you. Please sit down."

Her shopping rapidly dealt with and stowed away under the

table, Lucy found herself sitting down and having coffee ordered. "Thank you. I always come in here for coffee on market day, it doesn't get crowded like the other places. Only it isn't market day, but I happened to come into town for some shopping. . . ."

And to have her hair done, she didn't need to say. It looked terrible, ruthlessly sculptured into a fashionable shape that made her face strained. She was beginning to realize that the two expensive dresses she had just bought probably suited her even less. She could compete with Mirabelle and Bunty only on her own level, and already she was losing there.

"The village, I mean. It's a sort of tradition to call it the village, even though it's a town. I called yesterday, actually, but they said you were away all day. Bunty asked me to see you. . . . well, to drop in as I was here."

"Bunty," Henry repeated, politely puzzled. "Bunty. Let me see. . . ."

"Yes, my husband's cousin. Miss Meacham. She lives by the river, she binds books. Small and quick, like an elf. Oh, God, I've got the wrong man. . . ." Lucy looked around wildly, scrambling herself together to rise.

"No, you haven't," Henry said, trying not to smile. "I know who you mean. I had to think for a moment."

"Did you?"

"You sound surprised."

"Do I? It's just that . . ." Lucy floundered and steadied herself by reciting, "She doesn't think she can have your book ready this week. She can send it on to you when it's finished, if you'll give me your address."

From the corner of his eye Henry saw the waiter approaching. "You're from the north, Mrs. Deane, aren't you?"

"Yes. So are you. I can tell by your voice. Where from?"

"Lancashire. And you?"

"Yes. Me, too." The waiter put down the tray and went away. Lucy arranged cups and poured coffee. Put at ease by Henry's manner and pleased to share common ground, she chattered happily. From time to time there was a wistful note in her voice, which prompted Henry to ask, "Would you like to go back?"

"Oh, no," she said quickly. She was not built for adventure or independence; there was only one place she could go back to, and that contained her mother. The humiliation would be dreadful. Her happiness blighted, she looked away from Henry, fingered her coffee cup and frantically searched for a change of subject in a mind all at once clogged by anxieties.

He left her to her awkward silence. He had no doubt she had been briefed with certain questions which, at any moment, impelled by her sudden tension, she would recall. She had the essential qualities of a go-between: innocence and stupidity; but in using her, Bunty, with characteristic arrogance, had overplayed her hand. Because Lucy was vulnerable. No woman in a state of permanent inner dismay was safe. No matter how ignorant, she would know *something*, and her own need for reassurance would make the little she knew accessible.

Collecting herself, Lucy sat up and squared her shoulders. Adopting a genteelly inquiring attitude that would have been painful if it had not been so funny, she asked artificially, "Are you having a pleasant holiday? The country around here is extremely . . . pleasant. I suppose you've been exploring interesting places."

"Yes," Henry agreed, with a smile.

"Yes. There are a great many interesting places. Did you go anywhere specially interesting yesterday?"

He nodded and smiled again.

She leaned forward brightly. "Oh . . . where?"

"Just here and there, you know."

"Oh, good . . . Did you have a particular reason for choosing this part of the country? Is there something particular you're interested in?"

He frowned at her interrogatively. She moved her hand in a gesture stiffly indicative of her grasp on her subject, herself and

—possibly—him. "Well . . . architecture, or flowers, or things. I often wonder when I see visitors about what's made them decide to come here. I mean, why here? I ask myself."

"It's a pleasant place to relax for a while, to forget all the everyday cares."

"Yes. Oh, yes, it's very relaxing. Very quiet . . . off the beaten track. Even at this time of year—or later on, when everywhere gets crowded—there aren't many visitors. Well, we're quite a long way from a main road that actually goes anywhere; and the railway closed down quite some time ago, I believe. There's nothing here, you see. Except interesting places, of course."

"Of course."

"Perhaps you have friends here?"

"No. I don't know anyone at all."

"Ah . . . No. I believe you're interested in books."

"Yes. Are you?"

"No, I know nothing at all about them," Lucy answered desperately. Remembering herself, she reached out with a kind of submerged panic to reclaim her politely inquisitorial air. "Of course, as they're my husband's business, I'm learning a little. It's really surprising how quite rare books turn up all over the place. I suppose you've had some fascinating finds. I'd be very interested to hear about them. Do you specialize in anything?" When he looked at her with pleasant incomprehension, she leaned forward. "Er . . . magic, for instance?"

"Oh, no."

"Oh, I thought—" and she thought theatrically for a moment, frowning for effect. "Didn't Bunty mention you had an interesting book on magic? Something quite rare. Where did you manage to find it?"

"Serendipity."

"*Where?*"

"That's the art of making happy discoveries. I just happened to come across it. I haven't got it now."

"Oh . . ." Brought to a dead stop by the unexpectedness of this,

Lucy stared at him. She didn't know in which direction to proceed next, and she did not need his charmingly forgiving smile or the amused look in his eyes to tell her she had made a total mess of getting anywhere. It was only the faintest consolation to her that Bunty, who was clever and actually knew what she was doing, had failed as well. And she was grateful to him for telling her what "serendipity" meant, otherwise she would have triumphantly carried the word back in the belief that it was a geographical location. Bunty would have brained her.

Henry said, "It's odd she should mention it to you."

"Oh, why?"

"Well, when I spoke to her about it, that evening I took her to dinner, she didn't even remember it."

"But you didn't speak to her about it, you didn't tell her anything. She—" Lucy stopped, confused. Then, with a sigh, collapsed visibly into her normal self. "Oh, I don't know. I don't know anything. As a matter of fact, she really has got a terrible memory. Do you know, sometimes she forgets if she's had anything to eat. I suppose I must have sounded a bit rude, asking questions. I hope you didn't think so."

"Not at all. It's nice to talk to you."

"Do you find it a bit lonely? Being here on your own?"

"I do a little," he said, because her sympathy needed direction. And then, because her own loneliness was suddenly in the wilderness of her eyes, he added, "And you?"

"Oh, gosh, not a bit." She laughed bravely. "I've got lots of friends and so much to do. Of course, sometimes it's a bit . . . Well, I left it rather late to get married; I'm thirty-eight, you see. If I'd been younger, I suppose I'd have found it easier to adapt myself. But I'm a city girl, and the country . . . strangers . . . new ways . . . "

"How is it you come to be here, such a long way from home?"

"I didn't mean it to sound like that. It's lovely. I wouldn't change it, honestly. Well, I suppose it all sounds harebrained and improbable—for someone like me, I mean—but in the spring I just had an impulse to take myself off to the Festival at Marleigh. Do you know it?"

"Yes, I know Marleigh," Henry said.

Encouraged, Lucy talked about Roland and her meeting with him, lovingly distributing her favorite clichés about their courtship and marriage, her eyes bright and soft, her face relaxed in its generous happiness. She talked for a considerable time, gently prompted by Henry. The lounge gradually filled up with people coming in for coffee and after a while she grew aware of this, and looked at him guiltily. "Oh, I'm sorry, keeping you here, chattering away about my affairs. I expect you'll want to be out on this nice day. Are you going anywhere special?"

"I thought of the church. I haven't had a look at it yet."

"That's a good idea. I believe it's very interesting, very old."

"That means you haven't seen it. Will you come with me? We could look at it together."

"Oh . . . well."

"Please. Give a fellow northerner the pleasure of your company a little longer."

"Since you put it like that," Lucy said, returning his smile. She had little enough to do with her time, and it was a pleasure to her to be with someone uncomplicated who would gossip with her about ordinary things.

They stowed her shopping in her car and set off in the sunlight down the twisting streets to the edge of the village, where the fields opened out and the church stood.

"Did you know," Henry said, "that often early churches were built on sites that were particularly sacred to the old pagan religion?"

"No. How fascinating," Lucy said, trotting to keep up with his strides, glancing up at him with bright apology. "I'm afraid I don't know much about things like that."

"That means I've got a chance to show off," Henry said.

She laughed and said eagerly, "Yes. Do tell me. I'd like to know."

He told her briefly about the period of overlap when the old religion coexisted with Christianity. "Conversion wasn't instantaneous. A system of worship established over hundreds of years couldn't disappear overnight. A great deal of it was absorbed because people carried their beliefs and their customs and their gods into the new religion."

"It's wrong, though, that sort of thing. Wasn't it?"

"It was a matter of expediency, at first. As the church grew stronger, it became more dogmatic; eventually it was able to make churchgoing compulsory, to outlaw paganism and make adherence to it a punishable offense. But it lingered. It lingered on for hundreds of years. In a sense it's never died, although the forms in which it's expressed now are scarcely recognizable: dancing round the maypole, making corn dollies, superstitions about the moon and horseshoes, stories of fairies—"

"Oh—" Lucy interrupted, slowing in her busy trot.

"What is it?"

She remained quiet for a moment, her face rapt. Then she shook herself impatiently. "Something I've just thought of. It was what you said about fairies. . . . Nothing important. Silly, really."

"Try me."

"Oh, no . . . You really *would* think I was silly." They went up the steps into the churchyard, where the mysterious yews caught them in their somber shade. Lucy murmured, "I read somewhere that the real idea of fairies wasn't that they were little things with wings. They were ordinary-sized, but they were people who didn't quite . . . belong. They lured other people away, with lights, over marshes and through woods—"

"To steal their souls, Mrs. Deane," Henry said quietly as they stepped into the coolness of the porch.

She looked at him. "Yes. That was it, I remember now. . . . To steal their souls."

They went down the narrow aisle and Lucy followed Henry into a pew. It was a conventional action, a polite paying of respects during which, generally, Lucy's mind went blank with a kind of spiritual embarrassment. She had never known if she believed in God, and she didn't know now; but as she knelt in silence, some resolution came to her, a dawning belief in herself as a creature who would not always be duped and dismissed. She was aware, curiously, that this had something to do with the man at her side, and the confidence he gave her.

They looked around the church. It was Norman, Henry told her, with restorations and additions of a later date. The decorations were naïve and energetic, with recurring motifs of oak leaves and acorns. Lucy admired a knight and his lady at peace on a tomb chest and agreed with Henry that the stained glass in the south aisle was a little vulgar. All the while something tugged at her memory, troubling her until she realized what it was: the box that held Bunty's crystal was carved with a design of the same leaves. She said nothing of it and went with Henry to the font. "It doesn't seem very *religious*, does it?" she said, after she had painstakingly examined it.

"But it is. Like the oak leaves. And older, much older than the religion worshiped here. . . ."

Time had worn the vigorous carving of the font. The skull had lost its terror, if it had ever had any; the ears of corn that once sprouted from its mouth and eye sockets had become pitted until they were scarcely recognizable, and the poignant symbol of death and renewal was going slowly back into stone.

"I think it's rather sad," Lucy said.

They went out into the sunlight once more and walked slowly around the church. They came to an untended part, where stumps of gravestones leaned drunkenly and grasses and thistles grew tall. "The north side," Henry said. "Traditionally—according to the Christians—it belonged to the devil. That was the door—there. It's been filled in."

"Why?" Lucy asked, with only a momentary twinge of uneasiness at the recollection of another blocked doorway.

"To the pagans, the north was rather mysteriously a place of power, the hub of the universe. The great goddess had her starry castle at the back of the north wind. So the people who were forced to come to church—because it was often dangerous not to be seen worshiping in the accepted manner—came and went by the north door, as a secret tribute to their goddess."

"But it couldn't stay a secret—the priests found out—and it was blocked up. I see. . . ."

They waded through the unkempt grass and stood in the small, dim porch. The dankness touched Lucy's skin and she shivered. She peered up to study the decoration above the door. The light was bad and it took her some moments of murmuring, "What an odd thing . . . I can't quite make out . . ." before she gasped and stood in utter silence, her face congealed in an expression of disbelief.

A woman was carved above the doorway. Enduring, neglected, she sat in a posture shocking to Lucy's eyes, disturbing to Henry's, sacred to the people who had placed her there. Her legs open, her sexual parts emphasized, her candid laughter undimmed, she crouched up in the shadows, making her challenge and her offering to time: her unchanged, ever changing pleasure and fertility.

Lucy stepped back, cannoned into Henry and went threshing out among the gravestones. Shock dislocated her sense of direction; she walked fast, in circles, the blush beneath her tan making her skin vivid as a rose. Too embarrassed to speak directly to Henry when he caught up with her, she muttered about disgraceful things that shouldn't be allowed. Then, because she could not escape from him, or herself, she almost accused him, asking in a hurt voice, "Did you *know* it was there?"

"No. But I suppose I should have guessed. Bunty hinted at something."

"Oh. Bunty. She *would.* That's the sort of thing that would amuse her. The *effect* it has, I mean. She has no sense of decency."

Henry stopped Lucy decisively. He stopped her by grasping her arm and forcing her to stand still and face him. "Look at me,

Mrs. Deane, and for God's sake don't be embarrassed. We're grown-up people. That was just a piece of stone; we've seen worse written on walls."

"I suppose so." She looked at him reluctantly, very briefly, and then tugged away, trying to launch herself once more into flight. He kept his hold on her arm and made her walk slowly. After a while, when she had begun to collect herself, he released her. "But on a *church* . . . put there *deliberately.*"

"I could explain it to you, but I don't think you're in quite the mood to listen."

"My God, you're right," Lucy said.

"You dislike Bunty?"

"I hate her," Lucy said wildly. Her distress made her unsteady and she needed to talk it away. In the process she revealed something of Bunty and a great deal of herself. When her bitterness and humiliation had worked to the surface, and Henry had patiently taken account of it all, she repeated, "I hate her. . . . No, I don't. In an awful way I admire her—her arrogance, her poise. She frightens me a bit. And Mirabelle. I really can't take the two of them on."

Henry said carefully, "I thought Mirabelle was in America."

"She's come back. Suddenly. Bang, just like that. In the middle of the garden. My garden. One minute she wasn't there, then I blinked and she was. I don't expect you to believe me, but that's what happened."

"I believe you. And doesn't it depend what's at stake?"

"What?"

"Taking them on."

They were in the shadow of the yews. Lucy paused in her fussy step. For a moment her face was stiff with the effort of assessing her anxieties, then it broke open helplessly. She gulped, "I'm sorry. I think I'd better go now," and began to fumble in her handbag, turning, hesitating, her tears glittering silver in the dark green shade.

"No, you mustn't go home like this," Henry said gently, passing her his handkerchief. "They'll wonder what I've done to you."

"Oh, it isn't *you.* You're very kind. It's awful, behaving like this in front of a stranger."

"Think of me as a friend, then it'll be all right. I'll tell you what. There's a path across the fields. Let's go along there to the fort."

"Fort?" Lucy repeated stupidly, trying to cope with the change of subject.

"Yes. An iron age fort, or settlement. There's nothing much left of it now but it's very peaceful there. A nice walk will make you feel better. Come along, and I'll tell you something."

"Is it a secret? No one ever tells me those," Lucy said dismally. She managed to suggest that if he did he would only add to her burdens.

"In a way." Henry watched her blow her nose and wipe her eyes on his handkerchief, apologetically stuffing it away in her handbag with a promise to wash it and return it to him. He had calculated her use to him as an ally, an innocent and generous ally; an appeal of a certain kind would do it. And it did not need to be entirely true.

14

"I KNOW why Bunty sent you," Henry said, as they set off across the fields.

"I wish *I* did."

"You're just saying that to make me feel better. It's all right. I don't mind admitting it."

"I'm not," Lucy said, intrigued. "Admitting what?"

"The rejected-suitor bit. The way I feel about Bunty, the way she's been leading me a dance. I can see she's been a little too clever, though, sending you to check up on me, to see if I'm still interested or if I'm going to admit defeat. The male ego's easily dented. It wouldn't occur to her that I'd admit as much to you, though."

"I didn't know. Honestly, I didn't," Lucy said, her face glowing with delight. This was something she could understand, sympathize with; perhaps she could even help.

"Didn't you?" Henry looked skeptical. "I suppose I have tried to rush her a bit, although she must be used to grown men turning into adolescents and chasing her all over the place."

"*Did* you? So *that's* why she's been hiding at our house. I had a feeling she was keeping out of someone's way."

"I tried telephoning, and going to her house. I've looked for her all over the place," Henry said, with some truth. "And all the time she was with you."

"*Most* of the time," Lucy said, at pains to be accurate. "She comes and goes. It's a bit bewildering, really. Since—let me see —Saturday."

"That was the day after I met her. . . ." Henry gave a selective account of his meeting with Bunty and his evening with her. "There isn't anyone else, is there? She said there wasn't."

"Oh, no. Not now. As a matter of fact—let me try to sort this out—*that* . . . er . . . the other man there used to be had something to do with the day you met Bunty, in a remote sort of way, if you're who I think . . ." Lucy said incoherently. She was trying to be tactful and at the same time reexamine in her mind the afternoon Bunty had turned up. She had been in a confused state then, and the time lapse only made things worse. She tried to remember what Bunty had said about mistaking someone for an inquiry agent.

"Please," Henry said, looking down at her tortured expression. "That first day my tracks crossed with Cedric's. If that's what you're trying to *avoid* saying, please stop before you tie yourself in knots."

Lucy's face cleared. "Oh, you know. Thank heavens. Bunty

was in something of a state . . . well, she must have been, to come chasing round to us, and that would have accounted for it. Frankly, I was in a state myself; that's why I've got it all mixed up. I was so shattered when she suddenly appeared—and then to find out who she was . . ."

Letting Lucy chatter on, Henry tried to imagine Bunty in "something of a state." It was impossible. So talked of, her fleeting presence invoked, she moved on the air about him with the sweetness of her scent, the glancing movements of her small, gainly body; and always slipping out of reach, always cool, she challenged him with her self-possession, her primitive knowledge of herself. To Lucy, who plainly had a romantic heart, he had presented an unalarming version of his response to Bunty; the truth of it would have shocked her speechless.

Then he realized what Lucy was saying, and interrupted her. "You mean you didn't know she was your husband's cousin?"

Lucy answered no in a subdued way. She didn't want to have to admit how little Roland told her about anything. Simulating an intense interest in the hawthorn hedges that bordered the track, she said casually, "There was a family quarrel. Some time ago. They've made it up now. But really"—her voice took on a note of reluctant admiration—"she is a cheeky thing. She's not avoiding you at all. She can't be, sending me to find out who you are and why you're here. . . ."

"I'm on holiday," Henry protested. "Doesn't she think I am?"

"She said—I do remember this—not to me, of course, to Mirabelle, 'He's either a completely innocent bystander or something cataclysmic. Anyway, he's as close as a bloody oyster.' "

"I don't *feel* cataclysmic."

Lucy laughed. "Of course not. How can anyone? Honestly, I don't understand what they're talking about half the time. And all that silly stuff about a book, just because it belonged to that mad old conjurer or whatever he was. Who cares where you got it?"

"Who indeed? And anyway, I haven't, now."

Lucy hesitated. "No. Er . . . I suppose she'll ask, so would you mind telling me where it is?"

"I don't know. It's gone."

"Do you mean you've lost it?"

"I must have. I can't think of anyone who would want to steal it, can you?"

"No," Lucy said, although from what she had heard from Roland, it seemed to her that the book trade reverberated with accusations of every kind of dishonesty, and theft appeared to be commonplace in a game where everyone cheated. "But shouldn't you inform the police?"

Several times in his mind Henry had reviewed the bizarre circumstances surrounding his loss of the book. The mere thought of turning these into official language made him wince. He smiled and shrugged. "I couldn't even say when it disappeared. And it's not important; just a curiosity I picked up. I didn't understand it anyway. I suppose Bunty was interested because it was in the family, so to speak."

"Oh, I suppose so."

"Do they talk much about him?"

"Not a lot. Well, would you? I think I'd keep jolly quiet about him," Lucy said scornfully, forgetting she had done nothing of the sort.

They had reached the stile at the end of the track. Henry went first and Lucy followed, clambering ungracefully, catching her skirt, wobbling about as she grappled with her handbag. Henry reached up, lifted her clear and put her on her feet as carefully as if she were a child. The moment before he released her, she assessed him in an entirely feminine way, not with her mind but with her senses: his tall, hard-muscled body was capable and controlled, he was gentle and completely male and Bunty was off her head not to want him.

It was just a short way then to the clearing and the great raised circle that was all that was left of a place where people had fought and lived and died. Grass had long since covered it, wild flowers bloomed, and its stillness now was disturbed only by their voices, the sound of the birds and the whispering movement of the trees that had grown up around it. The ditch had become filled in and was no more than a depression, rising gently to the platform which lay at the base of the rampart. They walked around the outer face to a gap that Henry explained had once been the entrance, with stout wooden gates and perhaps a wooden bridge over the top. The entrance formed a passageway, opening out to a sheltered clearing where, scattered about, the shapes of hut circles could still be seen.

They clambered to the top of the broad rampart and sat in the sunshine. Lucy looked about contentedly: there were none of the blocked doorways and rude carvings and appearing and disappearing people that went toward making her life such a hazard. She said, "I like it here. You're right, it is peaceful . . ." and for a while talked sympathetically with Henry about the disappointments of love. Then she glanced at her watch and he said quickly, "Oh, don't say you've got to go. I was going to ask you to have lunch with me."

"Oh, thank you, but I'm sorry. I have things to do at home. I can stay a little while longer, though. This afternoon we're going to a garden party, Roland and I—Mirabelle, too, I think. But not Bunty. It's her day for teaching at some college or other, or I'd have got you an invitation. And this evening we're going out somewhere, I'm not sure where. But listen, let me see. . . . Friday, will you come to dinner?"

"That's very kind of you."

"No, no, not at all." She was eager in her enjoyment of conspiring with him. "Bunty's sure to be there; she always seems to be now. Anyway, I'll make sure. I'll ask her specially. But I won't tell her about you. There." With satisfaction, Lucy laid her small plot. She might have hesitated had Henry been less calm, less assured. Even if Bunty was furious (or pretended to be), Lucy was confident he could manage the situation, and she couldn't resist the temptation to help matters along. "Of course, Mirabelle might be there, too. But that won't matter, will it?"

"Not at all. I look forward to meeting her," Henry murmured.

"Good," Lucy said, nodding in a pleased way.

Henry saw how necessary it was for her to commit herself to something, even a small matter—although to her it was an important matter, presenting her with opportunities to be decisive and managing. He had never known a woman whose emotions were so easily accessible, skimming across the surface of her personality: he had seen how quickly she was hurt, quickly comforted; how dismay, indignation, curiosity took possession of her features the instant they occurred; how readily her generous mouth smiled. But he sensed in her a reserve of strength of which she was herself probably unaware: because—he pondered—it had never been tested? Or because all her resources were being used by some trial she had to endure alone?

"You know, when you're attracted to someone you seem to see them in a certain way . . . things that are there but other people can't see . . ." Lucy said, talking in a guarded strain at some length while Henry murmured encouraging agreements, wondering what she could be leading up to.

"Do you think Bunty's a little bit odd?" she asked, at last coming to the point.

Henry didn't answer at once. She turned to him, anxious he should understand, fearful she might offend him. He looked into her trusting brown eyes. "Yes."

She gave a sigh. "Yes. If I tell you something, please don't repeat it to anyone else; they'd think I was silly. . . . It's Mirabelle, too, and Roland when he's with them. I didn't notice it separately, but once they were all together. . . . We were having dinner, you see, one evening, and it wasn't like any evening I'd ever known. It was as if they'd affected it, all of it: the atmosphere, the color of the dark, the scent of flowers from the garden, the food. Everything was—please don't laugh—*more* than it had ever been. There was something at the back of my mind, some way of—not explaining it—pinning it down, something I couldn't grasp. Then, when you said about fairies—*that* was it. The stories you read when you're a child, about a mortal meeting a mysterious person and being taken to a place where there's feasting and laughter and beautiful people—and then, then it all vanishes, and the mortal wakes up in the ordinary world."

"Did you?" Henry asked, smiling. When she hesitated, and gave him a half-ashamed glance, he asked again, "Did you?"

"Yes. That is . . . I must have gone to sleep. I don't *usually* do that on guests, you know. When I woke up, the candles had gone out, the table was cleared. There was no one there, not even Roland. There was no one in the house at all."

"What did you do?"

"It was quite late. I—I went to bed."

"When did he come back—your husband?"

Lucy shook her head and murmured that she didn't know, she must have fallen asleep. Henry, who had recognized in her the need to talk of matters that bewildered and possibly frightened her, also recognized her reluctance to pursue those matters any further. Nevertheless, he persisted, on a note of casual interest. "The next day, though. Didn't you ask where they'd been?"

"Oh—they said they'd had something to do. . . . I told you, they're a bit odd. Oblique," Lucy said, wondering to herself how she had come across a word so appropriate. Because that was what they were, and that one word contained all the qualities she couldn't express to Henry: the casual voices holding a whisper of contempt she strained unavailingly to catch; the clever faces, turned coolly to assess her, masking secrets she would never uncover; the bodies poised on a self-assurance so delicate that even as she held them fast in her anxious gaze there was the sense that imperceptibly they were sliding away somewhere else.

Henry left her to her silence. After a while she murmured, "I must go soon," but sat on, without moving.

Henry, lying relaxed on the bank, looking up at the blue summer sky, twisting a stalk of grass between his fingers, murmured,

"This is a strange part of the country. I don't think I've ever been anywhere quite like it, you know. There's so much a sense of the past that after a while time becomes meaningless, there's just a feeling of continuity, of roots going back a long, long way. . . ."

Lucy said timidly, "I thought it was my imagination at first, because I wasn't used to old buildings, and the silence, and all these trees . . . but it's true. You think sometimes that anything could happen here, because this is the right place for things to happen. Bunty and Mirabelle *belong* here. Oh, they could live in other places, but here they're—let me see—*realized.* It's not the same for Roland—almost, but not quite. I don't know why."

"Bunty's family have always lived here, haven't they? She told me. Her mother, her grandmother, her great-grandmother . . . down there in those houses by the river, generations of them."

"Yes. Mirabelle's, too. And there are other people—people they know—just the same. I wonder if that's what makes them so—so sure of themselves. Because this is their place and always has been, and they can trace their line right back to . . . to . . . How far would it go?" she asked, turning a perplexed gaze on him.

"Back to the beginning. When this was a very sacred place."

"Was it? That explains it, I suppose," Lucy said, thinking of Nine Maidens, the river and the wood, and looking around the fort, which, with its sweep and its seclusion, expressed the religious unity of it all, slumbering entranced in a fold in the landscape.

"Some things are never forgotten," Henry said, watching her face.

"No. It makes you a bit . . . uneasy. Not," she added, forcing herself to be bright, "that it should. Not that there's any reason."

"If ever there were, you know where to find me," Henry said.

IT had been a surprisingly happy day for Lucy: the morning with Henry, the afternoon at the garden party with Roland. When the evening grew disorganized by too many people, by surges of movement that resulted in drinks somewhere, and dinner somewhere else, and drinks yet again somewhere else, she went on being happy. All the necessary ingredients were present: laughter and talk and Roland. She asked for nothing more. If most of the faces about her were unfamiliar, they were friendly, and she responded eagerly to them; if Bunty and Mirabelle found her lack of elegance and social polish amusing, they concealed it very well.

Late in the evening, Lucy found herself back in her own home, cheerfully playing hostess to company that thronged the rooms and spilled out into the garden. Her only regret was that Henry was not there—an efficient conspirator would have somehow contrived his presence. She had given Bunty a rather wandering account of her meeting with him, overplaying apologetic meekness until Bunty's carefully controlled patience splintered into exasperation. "All you had to do was give him a message and ask him a few questions, not bleed to death. I wish I'd never bothered. For God's sake, shut up, will you."

Lucy, hugging her romantic secret to herself, thought during the evening that if she had managed things properly, Bunty would not be circulating with the quicksilver and provocative air that struck terror into the hearts of women who dared not trust their husbands; she would be sitting somewhere in the moonlight with Henry, holding hands and being an entirely different person.

When the guests began to leave, a large girl called Daphne revealed herself as being helplessly, though amiably, drunk. Lucy worried about coping with her, or disposing of her, but no one else seemed to mind. People said good-naturedly, "Daphne's at it again . . ." indicating that she made a habit of it. She collapsed onto Bunty, who buckled under the weight, shouting urgently, "Daph, can you go home?" Daphne replied solemnly that she could, it would be all right: "Daddy's on tour."

"Is he an actor?" Lucy asked, hovering.

"No. A high court judge," Bunty panted. "And a strict teetotaler."

Daphne said carefully, "You have such a hell of a job explaining me."

"We have a worse one moving you. Daph, you're a dear girl but don't pass out yet. . . . Help!"

Eager hands disentangled them. Bunty emerged to be patted and smoothed by Mirabelle while Daphne was passed into Roland's care. There were two more guests to help him. Lucy saw them all off in Roland's car and when the good nights and door-banging and noise of cars at last died away, she went back across the yard, her head full of voices and laughter.

As she walked, the night folded about her and only the trot-trot of her high-heeled sandals marked a passage through the silence. In one instant she was aware of the broken slabs of stone beneath her feet and recollection swooped on her of the sunlit afternoon when she had trodden the same ground and something unknown had sped beyond the boundary of her vision.

The next instant a shock traveled through her, wrenching her entire body. Some distortion of sound that might have been her own voice rang in her head before her consciousness reeled. She was buffeted, riven, scorched; creatures and objects sped grotesquely, glancing, writhing, consuming others and themselves. She had an awareness of the elements fusing and splitting asunder, hurtling her unseen enemy beyond the steeps of time.

Then everything vanished. The night expanded, dark on dark;

her heart stopped beating, her breath was extinguished, blackness pressed against her eyelids, and she hung in the chasm of space.

There, she endured. Smaller than the speck of the farthest star in the vast, rocking emptiness; but she endured. And the danger eddied and ebbed and went into the hand of death.

She was standing in the yard, the night air floating with the scent of honeysuckle. Her body was rigid, her hands clasped together; she was talking, talking her way back to reality, pouring out the language of nightmare before it was forgotten. Then she stopped with a gasp, on an inward collapse, and stared at Mirabelle.

Mirabelle, standing close, had taken Lucy's hands between her own and was holding them. Lucy cried, "Didn't you feel it?" and Mirabelle answered, "No, he can't reach us. We're too strong for him, much too strong."

Wonderingly, Lucy felt against her fingers the silky fabric of Mirabelle's dress, the adamant bone between the downy breasts, the beat of the heart. She had no notion of time. She did not know how long she had been talking to Mirabelle, her hands enclosed in the cool, firm grasp; how long Mirabelle had used her body to absorb the terror and confusion.

There was only one thought in Lucy's head; it had been there all the time and it was as insane as anything that had happened to her: it was the thought of Henry. In her distracted state she had accepted the thought, she had even acknowledged its association with danger; but as soon as she made the effort to impose order in her mind, her mental habits established themselves, driving her to look for the comfort that was rightly hers in the place where it rightly resided.

Roland. If Roland had been there, this terrible thing would never have happened. If Roland had been there, she would not now be at the mercy of these awesome, mysterious women.

She wrenched herself from Mirabelle, almost colliding with Bunty, who put a hand out to touch her arm. "Leave me *alone*,"

Lucy cried. "It's all your fault. These awful things only happen because you're here. . . ." She was half running toward the house, but she couldn't escape. They accompanied her, shapes gliding in the dark, Bunty saying, "That's not true. They're happening because you're here. Can't you see—it's you. . . ."

But Lucy wouldn't listen. In the house, she hurled herself at the stairs, tripping on her long dress, scrambling upright. She had an irrational faith that they wouldn't follow her upstairs. Upstairs was private territory; to her knowledge they had never trespassed.

She was so isolated by her distress she scarcely knew what was happening. Fleeing from them, she found herself in her room and shut the door. She switched on the lamp and then pressed her hands over her face. She heard her name called, footsteps, the click of the door; but she stood like a child playing a game, hiding her face: if I can't see you, you can't see me. . . .

"Lucy," Bunty said.

Lucy looked at her. It seemed to take a long time, and everything swayed.

"Sit down. . . ."

Managed by Bunty's cool little hands, Lucy sat. She seemed to have no will left. She had shut her mind to what would inevitably happen, and the effort of staying blanked off so closed her into herself she was only distantly aware of Mirabelle's presence, of a glass with brandy in it, of voices and perfume whispering about her.

There was the sting of brandy in her throat; the glass was empty. She let it fall and dully watched it roll on the rose-patterned carpet. Bunty's foot extended, tiny, high-arched, the nails glittering with coral varnish, the bare, suntanned skin crossed by the jade thongs of her sandal. She put her toe to the glass and tapped it away under a chair, so that no one should tread on it.

After regarding this action, and the completion of it, Lucy leveled her gaze upward. The glow from the pink-shaded lamps caressed the room: the frills, the ribbons, the rose-pink this and dainty that. Lucy's room was the most feminine, the prettiest that anyone could imagine; and it was all hers, and only hers.

Lucy lay alone in her bed, her eyes open but glazed between sleeping and waking. She had refused to speak to Bunty and Mirabelle; silence was the last stronghold of her pride. She had shut her mind against them and turned her head from them, in fear of the contempt on their faces, and at last they had gone away. After a while Roland came home. She heard the blur of voices from below, reaching her through layers of darkness, baffled by the brick and stone of the old house.

For days her secret dread, scarcely admitted even to herself, had been that Roland had already told them. But Bunty's questions (automatically her mind cut out the tone of it; she had recorded the words, that was all)—"Lucy, why don't you sleep with Roland?"—proved that he had not done so. Loyalty? Respect? Or simply because she was of so little account the matter was not worth mentioning? She had no doubt that in that dreadful partisanship, all manner of things could be said; but how would he speak of it to them when he would not discuss the matter with her?

When they had first been married they had talked; not very much, it was true. The first disappointment was remote, clouded by unfamiliarity. With her woman's instinct to preserve his pride, she had confined herself to agreement: yes, they were tired, not used to each other, her experience was limited, there was plenty of time.

There was all the time in the world, she learned, for her gentle, murmuring encouragements, her timid caresses, her seductive nightdresses, her scent, her strategies. Endless nights to lie beside him as he slept, her mind bruised by her body's rejection. For the woman who could not rouse her husband there were centuries of humiliation, eons of despair.

Her sense of decency held her together. She refused to whine;

the demand "Desire me" would, by its very crudeness, destroy the response it sought. But day by day, night by night, her confidence warped, and while there were still some remnants of it left, she forced herself to speak to him.

They were taking an evening walk, strolling along the tree-enclosed lanes. Lucy had keyed herself up to say what had to be said. Her heart lurched and her nerve ends screamed. When at last she burst out, "Roland, we can't go on like this," his puzzled look, his blank, "Like what?" told her he had no idea what she meant. "Not having any sex—" "Oh, really," he interrupted. "It's not like you to make a fuss about something so unimportant. What does it matter when we get along so well?" His light tone dismissed her; rather than force him toward a pain that perhaps existed in him, too, she took the blame on herself. "I'm not making a fuss. I feel I've failed you." "No, you mustn't think that. I love you. You're my downy brown little Lucy, you're everything I want. There, does that make you feel better?" The "little Lucy" reduced her to the status of a petulant child; if she had been honest she would have said so, but her courage failed her. On the edge of hysteria, she nodded and was silent, fearing to lose the little she had.

In attempting to put things right, she had somehow made everything worse. From that moment he retreated farther from her, shrugging away her most innocent touch, avoiding her good-morning kiss. She grew close to a realization of herself as something repulsive and pathetic and dared not continue to sleep with him in the insulting intimacy of the double bed for fear her tears should betray her. When she said one day, "Roland, do you think it would be a good idea if I used the pink room?" it was all she needed to say. There were no questions, heart searchings, protestations. Roland answered on just the right note of indulgent agreement: "Why, yes, Lucy, if you'd like to. . . ." There was no need for any delay for decorating or refurnishing; the room was all ready and waiting. It had been waiting ever since she moved into the house.

The voices below her changed in volume, threading through the labyrinth of her thoughts. She imagined she heard laughter, and Bunty's voice wailing something in a tone close to outrage. She got up and went to the window. After a while, she saw the two women going down the garden, moving in their weightless way, like ghosts in the moonlight. They were going home through the wood; Mirabelle, Lucy had discovered, owned a house next door to Bunty's. Neither Mirabelle nor Bunty bothered with the small courtesy "You must come and see me sometime." Lucy had a premonition that now they would ask her. A shiver touched her flesh. She wouldn't go.

She heard Roland on the stairs. When he reached the landing, she was at her open door, waiting. "Roland . . . did they tell you what happened? Down there in the yard?"

He gave her a bitter, oblique look. "Yes."

"I suppose you're going to tell me not to worry about it, that it was nothing . . . but this time *they* were there."

"I don't want to talk about it now. I don't want you imagining things in the night, having bad dreams. Nothing's going to hurt you here."

His concern touched her heart. She made an impulsive move to go to him, instantly stilled, converted to an indecisive gesture of her hand. "I'm not afraid. Honestly. Will you talk to me about it tomorrow?" He nodded. She had no reason to believe him; he had betrayed her many times. She turned her mind from this. If she went on putting her trust in him, then eventually everything would come right. "But *they* frighten me."

He looked directly at her and she saw how white he was. "I'm not surprised."

She gasped, "But . . . not you . . . You belong to them."

"I belong to myself. Why do you women always talk in terms of possession?"

"I didn't mean they possessed you in that sense . . ."

"You don't know what you mean. I'll tell you, since you've paraded our private life . . ." He looked past her into the bedroom, his eyes hard as stone.

"Roland . . . I *didn't.* You don't think I wanted them to know."

"It's too late now." He crossed the landing and stood quite close to her, looking into her face. He spoke abruptly, with occasional sardonic emphasis but no intensity. "They make spells. Oh, they know how to—the women in their family have always known. Some of them were burned as witches hundreds of years ago. Before that they worshiped at stones and trees and wells. Their magic goes back to the beginning of time. But it's a bit outdated now, and there isn't much left of it. Nobody needs it to make the crops grow, or the sun rise; nobody needs their everlasting, primitive fertility. They're like children who've never grown up, children who live in a world all impressions and senses and bodies. They wouldn't accept my father's world, the superiority of the intellect; they contended with him until he died—and still he's stronger than they are. So they made a spell. Like spiteful children, they're making me pay for their failure. You, too. They put the spell between us."

Lucy followed every word, concentrating so hard on what he was saying her own thoughts ran unheeded, and when she tried to gather them they dissolved in a vapor of doubt. She stood for some time, unable to speak, looking into Roland's face. At last he said, "Go to bed. Go to sleep. Something must be done. Tomorrow, perhaps," and turned away.

16

"YOU can't go," Lucy said. "I've got a headache, and we should talk. You haven't said a word all morning and now you're suddenly going to go off and leave me and you won't be back until tomorrow."

"It isn't sudden," Roland said. "I've had this sale in my diary for weeks."

"Damn your diary," Lucy said gloomily. She sat at the table in the small breakfast room, her chin in her hands, surveying the remnants of their late lunch. Headache or no, wretchedness or no, Lucy ate. It was a response to a lifelong belief that no matter what crises overcame her, she had a chance of survival if she kept her strength up. "You can't go," she repeated stubbornly.

But Roland was collecting himself together: wallet, checkbook, keys. His car was already in the drive, his overnight case on the passenger seat. He organized himself with a neatness so obsessive there was no room in his tight, controlled little world for her; he might already be a hundred miles away.

She made a deliberate effort to reach him. "I couldn't tell if you loved them or hated them or needed them. When you're with them you take on their coloring—did you know? When there were just the two of us here I couldn't understand what it was about you that was different. I know now: you were incomplete. Whatever you feel about them, you need them to make you an entire person."

Roland said, "Do you know that this place was once a center of worship for the old religion?"

"Yes. I know."

"There's a tradition here that women still retain some of the sanctity of the great goddess. My father knew this was just a silly superstition; it pleased him to come here and prove it. If my mother had acknowledged his superiority . . . but she never would. She loved him, and that weakened her; that in itself gave him ascendancy. Bunty's mother, too; she was very wild but he dominated her. And Bunty and Mirabelle loved him, but they wouldn't let go of their stupid beliefs. I was the youngest; I was torn about between them all. When I was a child, my father didn't have much time for me; I was left to them. They spoiled me, they punished me, they cared for me or neglected me just as they pleased. Sometimes it was terrible, sometimes it was wonderful. . . ."

But always you were the weakest, Lucy finished silently for him. Last night there had been some comprehension of doubt; now her head ached dully and the pain obscured a conviction that he had got it all wrong, from the very beginning. But she was a creature of habit. Nothing in her life equipped her to challenge; she had no daring, no resources for judgment.

"Roland, it was a long time ago. If we love each other . . ." He could have her strength, what there was of it. Surely he knew that?

"I always had to do as they said—Bunty and Mirabelle. Because they were older, and cleverer, because they were *women* and always right. If I didn't, they used to pretend they'd worked a spell to make me invisible. I could speak to them, scream at them; they'd just stare straight into me and out the other side. I never dared to touch them. I wanted to kick them and beat them with my fists, but I never dared to. I don't know why—perhaps because I half believed I *was* invisible and my hand would go right through them; so I was afraid to try. Then Mirabelle would say, 'It's time we found that little beast. We don't know what he's up to. . . .' And they'd do this elaborate ceremony, all swaying and chanting. That was bad enough; it terrified me. But worse than that, right at the moment I was supposed to appear, they'd pretend it hadn't worked."

The lack of emotion with which he spoke distressed Lucy. She put her hand half over her face, guarding her understanding. The small boy, long ago, had pleaded and shrieked, pitting himself against the merciless and indulgent creatures who tantalized him with his own helplessness.

Roland left the room abruptly. Lucy sat listening to him as he moved about and then irresolutely got up herself and wandered into the dining room. She stood at the open French window, looking into the garden. It was a brilliant day, hot and still. The sweet peas tangled, the roses arched, the clematis twined, all the movement that was not movement hung upon the air: stem and leaf and petal printed on the golden afternoon.

In an overstealing awareness, her glance turned. From the

glossy shade of the laurels Mirabelle regarded her. Vivid as the masquerade roses before which she stood, Bunty smiled at her.

She turned and ran.

Roland called, "Lucy?"

"I'm not going to *speak* to them," she shouted, from the top of the stairs.

They had things to say among themselves. In voices pitched in varying tones of anger, impatience and scorn, they insulted each other with a sublime disregard for Lucy's presence. Shut in her room, she could not hear clearly, and did not wish to. As Roland went out, passing through the hallway, he called them barren mares. It was not the last word; Bunty shouted he was an unscrupulous sod.

Lucy spent a great deal of time doing soothing and unnecessary things: turning out closets, tidying drawers, sewing on a button here, a piece of lace there. She had chocolate to nibble, magazines to read, new nail polish to try. The occasional murmur of voices beneath her window told her that Bunty and Mirabelle were sunbathing on the terrace. She ignored them and continued to occupy herself, discovering with faint surprise that in the time she had been married to Roland she had learned to be alone.

There was a soft rapping on her door, to which she did not respond. Mirabelle entered and said, "We're going to have something to eat, Lucy. Do come down. Your headache's better, isn't it?"

"Yes," Lucy said, with some surprise, not knowing when the nagging pain had dissolved. She was standing in her slip, surveying some dresses she had taken from her wardrobe and spread on the bed. The white leather handbag she had used the day before also lay there. Among the contents she had spilled out looking for cigarettes and lighter was Henry's handkerchief: large and practical as a man's handkerchief should be, and yet, with that dandified touch so much a part of his character, colored the palest blue; and his initials in the corner: *H.B.* She must wash it, she thought, and give it back to him as crisp and fresh as he had handed it to her.

Mirabelle had drifted to her side and was standing composedly, her head tilted a little as she considered the dresses. She put out a shapely hand. "That's nice. Wear that," she said, and drifted away.

Lucy showered, brushed away the dreadful hair set that had survived from the previous day, and put on the linen dress Mirabelle had chosen. Its russet color gave her suntanned skin a richly silken look and deepened the brown of her eyes. She had bought clothes extravagantly in her despairing efforts to capture Roland's erotic interest. The texture and design of the linen dress had an elegant restraint she would never have imagined could appeal to her, and she could not remember when she had bought it, or where.

She knew she must speak at once and this determination somehow contained her, although the furtive twisting movements of her hands betrayed her distress. She had rehearsed what she would say and she spoke steadily.

"I'm not going to go. My place is with Roland. I know about the way you've influenced him, dominated him. Perhaps if he'd chosen somebody special—your sort of woman—you might have left him in peace. But I'm ordinary and dull. I can't be graceful and do brilliant things. I suppose I'm a real letdown, bad for the family image. You can't go on being beautiful and mysterious and enchanted with quite so much conviction when there's someone like me around, worrying about what the neighbors think and if Roland's got clean socks."

As she paused for breath, Mirabelle shook back her ash-blond hair and gave a startled, delighted laugh. Lucy ignored her and went on doggedly. "You're not going to drive me away. Whatever you do, however you try to frighten me, however you weave your . . . spells, I'm staying with Roland. I'll win one day, if I hang on. . . ."

Bunty said, "Lucy, what are you talking about?"

"You know, There was no reason why anyone should ever have found out about Roland and me. You were the only two who were likely to. These last few days, I hated the thought of you knowing. I used to wonder how I'd react, how I'd endure your . . . amusement, your contempt. But it was worse, much worse than that. You've been laughing at me, I suppose, for trying to keep a secret you knew all the time. I was ashamed that Roland wouldn't make love to me. It doesn't make me any less ashamed that you've put a spell between us to separate us. If I was a different sort of person, I'd be stronger than anything you could do. But I've found something out. I can endure anything rather than give Roland up; so you might as well know that."

She stopped speaking, with some relief. The unwavering stares of Bunty and Mirabelle made her self-conscious. She looked down at her tensely shifting fingers, then about the terrace, where food was distributed informally on trays and small tables.

Mirabelle unfroze slowly from the gracefully arrested act of serving a plate of salad and said, "Is *that* what he told you?"

"It's true, isn't it?" Lucy stated accusingly. She had said what she must say and her strength of purpose was already in retreat. A sense of unreality might have insulated her, but she was solidly aware of herself, of them, of the amazing fact that Bunty appeared to be speechless.

Mirabelle said, "He accuses us of all sorts of things; none of them are true. Well, not many. We would never come between husband and wife, would we?"

In response to the question, Bunty wrenched her gaze from Lucy and turned to Mirabelle. Her face was expressive of inner questioning: doubtful, a little guilty. Then it cleared and she said, "Never."

"Oh—you liars," Lucy said, and put the back of her hand against her mouth because her control had almost broken.

Unaffected by the insult, Mirabelle said, "We have to talk, but we might as well eat. Come along, have some salad. Bunty, what did Roland say to us yesterday evening?"

"Turd that he is, he hedged, prevaricated and bullshitted. Finally, he said that we—*we* had laid some evil on him to prevent him from consummating his marriage. And I don't know how he had the brass to stand there and say it because that is the last—*the last* thing we would ever do. *As he is well aware.*" Bunty ate lettuce noisily, like an angry rabbit, while Lucy stared at her. "*Furthermore,* the sod could not, or would not, account for the fact that if he can't rise to the occasion, at least he could give you pleasure in other ways. There are plenty, and he knows it, for God's sake. But just to ignore you . . ."

"Please . . ." Lucy said weakly.

"He's grotesquely selfish. Grotesque."

Mirabelle, her voice languorously scornful, said, "But do you know, I almost felt sorry for him. He was in such a stew; so confused, so *angry.*"

"He's been like that all his life: stewed and confused and generally bashing me because I'm the smallest," Bunty said. "I don't feel sorry for him, and I've got the scars from my childhood to prove it."

Lucy was eating mechanically. She felt like a guest who had wandered into the wrong party and would be asked to leave any moment. She could almost imagine, for an instant, that the light voices and casual manner masked a terrible fury; but she was in an overwrought state and things were beginning to make less and less sense.

". . . almost sorry for him," Mirabelle said. "Which should put one on one's guard. The more he makes a bid for sympathy, the more likely it is that it's someone else who deserves it."

"Are you trying to tell me you didn't know?" Lucy said tensely.

"Of course we didn't, until last night. And what we knew then was his angle."

Bunty swallowed and said something graphic and extremely crude about angles. Lucy reacted instantly. "This isn't a joke."

"Who's laughing? We aren't responsible for his loss of virility, but we've decided—Mirabelle's decided—that something must be done about it."

Outrageous possibilities of how they would attempt this occurred to Lucy; so outrageous she had to shut them from her mind. She looked at Mirabelle and asked, "Why did you come back?"

"Because I'm needed here. My father's influence hasn't dissipated as we imagined it had. We couldn't understand why it had become active again. We attempted to find out—"

"The first night. When I looked in the crystal, and you pretended you wanted me to tell you something. But you just wanted me to stay there quietly, hypnotized or asleep or whatever, out of your way."

"You'd only have been frightened, or asked questions. We needed to concentrate. We went down into the cellar. We tried various rites, even some of his—although his magic is entirely orientated to the male principle. Roland could implement a little of it, very little; he lacks daring and conviction. Whatever strength he had he drew from Father—"

Bunty interrupted with her wicked little laugh. "The sorcerer's apprentice."

"Exactly. After Father's death, he became completely ineffectual, but as he was committed to his belief in Father's superiority, he's gone on believing in it—and believing that some of it resides in him."

Lucy suddenly had a long vision, a telescopic view of years of conflict and reconciliation, of curses and spells and counterspells, of wary alliances and supernatural assaults. Some vagrant empathy with one (or perhaps all) of them gave her access to the understanding of how they would fight and forgive, rend and heal, love and despise, in their everlasting fight for supremacy. It was hardly surprising that when the man who had been at the center of this bizarre tournament died, all the contestants should retire and go their separate ways, devitalized by the collapse of their own intensity.

She said, rather angrily, "Has it occurred to you that what Roland really believes in now are ordinary, quiet things, like a happy life and a good marriage?"

"Probably," Bunty said. "And he's even managed to make a balls of that."

"Well, you don't seem to have had much success with whatever it was you were doing in the cellar. I suppose you're going to blame that on Roland."

Mirabelle said, "Not entirely. Two factors, both linked. First of all, we didn't take sufficient account of your part in this. We thought you had simply experienced some stray psychic effect; we didn't realize you were the catalyst. Second, Roland chose you and married you and brought you here as the woman of this house. But you're not. He's denied you that status, he's reduced you to a mere cipher—"

"You don't think he *wants* to," Lucy cried despairingly, setting aside her pride. "It's my fault. Somehow. I don't know much about these things; maybe he's not very highly sexed and I just don't excite him. Maybe my chemistry's all wrong."

"Chemistry," Bunty said with disgust. "Really, Lucy, you can be a prune. You should stop reading all those trashy women's mags. A cuddly, *womanly* thing like you . . . *that's* chemistry. And I'm not sure about Roland being highly sexed or not. I don't quite know what your standards are. We must have a talk about that sometime. But there was never anything wrong with his performance in the past, was there, Mirabelle?"

"No," Mirabelle agreed.

Somewhere, in the distant reaches of Lucy's being, a shock trembled and was stilled. She didn't ask how they knew; she would never ask. Mirabelle's pale eyes looked into hers and she turned away, talking at random to cover her confusion. "I don't see what difference it makes. . . . I don't see that I have a part in this. . . . Does it matter? About this influence still being here."

Bunty said, "You're the woman of this house. This is your territory. The magus tried to make it his own once—"

"He's dead," Lucy cried.

Mirabelle made a movement of her hand. For all its command, the gesture had a strange gentleness, the palm open and the long fingers spread, as if in appeal. "But the contest isn't over. That's what you must understand. It's being fought again. Through you."

It was the first foreshadowing of dusk. For so long their voices had ensnared her, she seemed as she moved about the house to be caught in an invisible, vibrating web of words. They had made none of the adjustments of persuasion and encouragement that would allow them to meet her on her own ground; she must meet them on theirs. This attitude, she understood in a bleak moment of satisfaction, was not an insult, it was an invitation: by conceding nothing of themselves, they allowed her the totality of herself.

She had ceased to resent Roland's desertion. At some lost moment she had even relinquished her stubborn belief that his presence ensured her protection. She had nothing to cling to, not even habit; the world was enormous and moving toward darkness.

Their voices drifted to her from the terrace; she paused and listened. Mirabelle said, "We had to weigh what to lose and what to gain. Roland can try; he knows what the price could be. He agreed." Bunty's voice, sounding amazingly small and forlorn: "Do you want to tell me, Mirabelle?" . . . "No, doll. It's best not." . . ."All right."

Lucy moved quickly. It seemed that the idea had been in her head all day but she had somehow mislaid the volition to act on it. She was clumsy with nerves and bumped into a small table in her flight from the dining room. She froze, listening exaggeratedly. There was no reason for them to investigate the source of the noise; they had been content to leave her to potter about between the terrace and the kitchen. Their conversation, interrupted now, resumed again with scarcely a pause.

In the hallway she hunched over the telephone. As the door of the dining room was in plain view of the terrace, she had not dared to close it, in case they should wonder and come to see what she was doing. She had merely pulled it to and it was solid enough to muffle any noise—although the sound of the dial, circling and recircling, seemed unnaturally loud. When at last Henry came on the line, she was afraid to speak normally and announced herself in a stage whisper. He answered levelly, without hesitation, "Are you all right?"

"Yes. Listen. I've only got a minute. What I've got to tell you will sound very strange and I can't explain."

"Go on."

"I'm going into the wood with Bunty and Mirabelle. There's something they have to do and I have to be with them. I don't think they mean me any harm, but I can't just walk out of the house with nobody knowing, and commit myself to something I hardly understand. I had to tell someone. . . ." She paused. That wasn't right. In the midst of such tremulous awareness of herself, her nerves exposed certain truths. "No. You. I had to tell you. I don't know why."

"Shall I come now, and stop you from going?" In his voice there was something utterly receptive; he absorbed what she told him, and the manner in which she spoke, without argument, without any of the conventional responses of disbelief. She felt the vastness of the distance between them, the cleared ground, uncluttered by the familiar and the commonplace, where the restraints that governed strangers no longer existed.

She said, a little sadly, "No. I must go. You see, it's important. I'm a little afraid because I can't trust them, I don't know how to. And they wouldn't let you interfere; they've sent Roland away."

"I'll come to the wood. I'll be there if you want me. Remember that. I'll be there."

"Thank you," Lucy said. She put the receiver down and moved quickly from its tiny, betraying *ting!* In the kitchen she put away plates and cutlery, clattering them noisily—partly to account for her absence, partly because her hands shook a little. After a while, she grew calmer and her thoughts engaged her; when she went back to the dining room, she didn't notice that the door stood half open.

17

THEIR bodies slid pale as moths over the density of each moon-imprinted shadow and their sandaled feet made no sound on the grass as they moved past the fountain and the sweet, hidden honeysuckle, down between the silver faces of the tea roses.

To the wood, to the boundary, to the rim of softly trodden earth that separated bushes from trees . . . It was here Lucy faltered. Her perplexed senses had at last sent out one clear signal: here, between one footstep and the next, hangs the burden of the night, its terrors and insinuations. Stop. Stop.

Her companions, moving silently beside her, sensed her hesitation. They turned, caught up her reluctance, encircled it and stood, graceful as dancers, regarding her.

"But what will happen?" Lucy whispered.

Mirabelle shrugged. Her body had an amazing eloquence: with a lift of the shoulders, an outward turn of the hands on their long wrists, it said all that was necessary of acquiescence to the unknown. Then she made a gathering gesture, seductive in its perfection and almost ceremonious in its courtesy, and as if a decision had been spoken aloud, the three women drew together and stood poised upon the movement that would carry them forward.

Lucy had time for one frantic, mortal thought before she went into the trees: *How did I come to be here at all?*

The darkness had so undone the familiarity of the wood and invested it with such ancient magic it lay in some vast, powerful dream, the moonlight gleaming through its wild, high, interlaced branches. There were people there, presences who moved with a gentle purpose, drawing her from her fear. Sometimes she closed her eyes; ignorance and uncertainty blundered loudly inside her body, drowning the murmuring, measured voices. The fire that burned with a scented flame shifted light upon shadow and movement on stillness; the moist air thickened and the trees breathed.

Bunty's hands expressed a preternatural strength. She knotted the handkerchief and the knot was intricate and triumphant: it severed and joined, it interrupted and overlapped, it endured; it was a twist in the thread of time. It was time. She stepped up to Mirabelle, her arms stretched before her, her wrists loosely circled by the handkerchief.

The long silver sleeves of Mirabelle's robe slid back as she reached out. She touched the knot and slowly moved the handkerchief, working it through her fingers, round Bunty's wrists, until she reached the knot once more. Then she slid her hands between Bunty's and they stood for some moments, looking into each other's eyes, speaking softly.

Lucy felt a pang. She knew what they were doing, she knew that it was necessary; but Henry, who perhaps did not understand the courage and the skill it took to do this dangerous thing, would struggle. She hardly dared to believe, as she looked at the two fragile women, that their strength was greater than his.

The physical movement, the ceaseless, subtle, invisible movement, began to quicken. The night answered to it and the air itself began to move, faintly, with a gathering force.

Somebody gave her flowers and told her in a gentle country voice to take off her sandals. As soon as her feet made contact with the ground, she felt the vibration, the merest tremor, rhythmic and distant.

She walked lightly, putting her toes down first and letting her heels follow smoothly. The feel of the earth was so vital her whole body answered to it. She whispered, "Oh . . ." and the sound of her own voice brought her one instant's pause. Now, if she was to turn back; now was the time.

Her unknown companions waited beside her, hung upon the fraction of time in which she made her decision. Her decision. She looked to left and right, seeing how serenely they waited, and as she turned her head she took in the knowledge of the ever-widening circle, the figures that glanced naked as pearls between and beyond the breathing trees, the animal masks nodding and weaving in their silent, loving, welcoming laughter.

They said, "In the circle you will be between the worlds."

She nodded, unable to speak, and, holding her flowers carefully, she walked forward. She didn't know what the flowers were. Their stems, tender with life juice, quickened the palm of her hand with a brittle caress; the petals transmitted their velvet colors to her through her fingertips.

Mirabelle and Bunty waited for her; their robes dazzled her and her eyes clouded. Green and silver, out of focus, glittered and merged, slid downward and spilled discarded on the ground. The white porcelain figurine of Bunty stood before her, untying the cord at her waist. Mirabelle's cool fingers unfastened her dress at the back.

Around them the figures hurtled even faster as they retreated: the circle was expanding, pushed outward by its self-generated force, and in its spinning center her body was completely, utterly alive, its nakedness a shout of sheer joy.

She turned instinctively so that she was aligned with the house, and lifted her face to the full moon. She offered the flowers, tentatively, stooped, and with a delicate movement placed them in a pool of milky radiance. She stood back; Bunty took her left hand, Mirabelle her right. They pressed her fingers softly, companionably, and she answered the pressure. She felt the generosity of their bodies and knew how her own had been dishonored. She might, perhaps, have said so—she was never sure:

I couldn't admit it. I pretended to myself that it was all my fault. He used my love to make me feel ashamed, of myself, my sex. I knew he was punishing me, punishing all women through me, and I let him do it.

And they, perhaps, answered: *You understand now, that's the important thing. And you know that we would never have made you suffer. There has always been a woman in the house: wife, mistress, mother, always giving and receiving. But the balance is so fine, the equilibrium maintained by mutual respect. . . .*

She said (did she say?): *What dreadful pride the magus had, fearing enslavement, the sacrifice of the will. He understood nothing, he sacrificed himself, growing so small and blind inside his power. And it was all wasted, his own demons humiliated him at last, his magic destroyed itself. There was only hate left, in Roland. Poor Roland.*

And they asked, with ironic surprise: *Can you forgive him? Won't your forgiveness be a very bitter thing for him?*

Oh, yes. But he must learn to accept it. . . .

Their words, if they had spoken, breathed away into silence. The whirling figures had gone, flung beyond sight; only the sense of their movement remained, a spinning rim mysteriously containing the circle of trees. The earth trembled to the thunder of approaching hooves; an eerie light crept down, a light that drained away color and, retreating outward from the center, gathered and shifted, increasing in density, re-forming until it found its shape.

Nine enormous stones reared about them, stones as old as time, majestic and sacred, bedded in the timeless earth.

A havoc of wind started up in the trees beyond the ring of standing stones and, swelling and spreading, buffeted great gusts across the clearing as tree answered tree, shrieking and screaming. The force of it rocked Lucy, tearing at her hair, howling about her head. She wanted to cover her ears but knew she must cling to the warm, human hands that clasped hers, left and right. The grayness fled, the wind was ripped open in a blast of time, and the pack burst into the clearing.

The wild hunt, baying and whinnying and panting in the ride that carried them across centuries: the tall hounds, red-eared, their mouths agape; the powerful, splendid mares, clashing the crescents of their silver hoofs; and in their center, a willow in the white light, the goddess. Her pale hair drifted like water, her skin gleamed deathly pale, and with lips as red as rowan berries she smiled her fatal, loving smile.

As their riot engulfed her, Lucy knew the animal scent rank in her nostrils, the wild breath hot on her naked body. She saw them wheel and turn and speed between the standing stones, and before they passed into a brilliance beyond consciousness, she saw her flowers in the hand of the goddess.

Henry left his car by the road, vaulted over the stile and went swiftly down the track toward the river, where the small stone houses slept gray in the hollow of the night.

As he walked he put his hand into his pocket and opened out the little packet he had made of a paper napkin. The salt spilled into his pocket, sticking to his fingers in coarse, homely grains. Salt . . . He smiled wryly up through the canopy of leaves to where the full moon rode across the sky.

He turned right at the dip of the track and with his loping, almost soundless stride, walked through the cluster of houses, pausing, listening, glancing into opened doorways and the lighted windows of empty rooms. The absolute silence was emphatic, like a presence that walked beside him. He had been prepared for it; but all the same it caught at the edge of the imagination, the undefended area where superstition bred.

He retraced his steps and, leaving behind the deserted houses, plunged down the track to the footbridge and into the wood.

Here, silence stood in columns between the trees, moonlight shivered upon leaves that turned to unknown purposes and shadows dredged the weirdness of the night. He paused in his stride and listened. He had an impulse to turn around, walk away and forget everything; but as he listened for some sound that would betray the whereabouts of the three women—*and God knows,* he thought, *how many others*—his uneasiness was displaced by the need for movement.

He began to walk, his pace quickening. Something in his mind told him he was walking in the right direction, but something outside his mind drew him on. He pushed aside branches that seemed to cling to him; they made sighing, sweeping sounds, looping around him and crashing back on themselves. Saplings and twigs and bracken snapped beneath his feet; he was aghast at the noise he was making but he couldn't slow down. He told himself that speed was essential, although he didn't know what path he was following, what his destination might be, what he would do when he reached it.

Then he ran into something. His impetus carried him into something from which he rebounded, gasping, the breath driven from his body. He lurched and almost fell, scooped himself round and sprang upright.

There was nothing there.

There was nothing before him on the overgrown track and no movement to either side. He tried again, cautiously, until something compelled him to fling himself forward. This time he was ready, and it was worse. A suffocating blackness grasped him, buffeted him brutally, and he was staggering back, tearing breath into his lungs, his head ringing.

He crouched, fighting back the nausea that threatened to overwhelm him. The curtain of the night hung unstirring about him, and still there was nothing before him but a space between two trees, a space through which he desired to go, which would not let him pass.

He waited, huddled like an animal at the mouth of its lair. The sweat dried on his body and the sickening vertigo passed. He had a terrible dread of attempting once more a passage through the hole in the blackness; but his will was stronger than his dread, he knew that, and held on to it, gathering his resources.

He had known they would try to turn him back; but this was not merely a temporary check, this was a concentration of their total magic, this was their challenge. They could keep all their secrets—except one, and that one secret they could be persuaded to yield if he took up the challenge now and pitted himself against their primitive sorcery. If he did not . . .

He studied the two trees. Climb one? He almost laughed aloud. Trees were sacred. The guardian spirits who kept them would break his bones or poke his eyes out.

Walk around the perimeter of the band of force, searching for a weakness? No, that was a very subtle cheat he recognized in time: he could spend the night searching and all the while the weakness would be in himself. That course was simply another form of defeat, the worst kind, the self-deceptive kind.

Find a place where the force was intersected by a dead tree? A *dead* tree. He must be mad. Gods dwelt in dead trees, wearing the hollow barks around their incorruptible sleep. His mind wrinkled away from the thought of wakening one of those.

The river? No. Water was sacred to them, too; suicide by drowning would be a humiliation to carry into eternity.

So . . . if he did not take up the challenge now, he must get up and walk away and everything would be wasted.

He was calmer. He had thought his way into their magic and admitted there was no way around it; no way for a man. (An insane moment: *drag*. Jesus Christ, no; the implicit mockery of transvestism invited reprisals. They'd let him in and do the job properly, and he'd come back minus his dearest possessions.)

He had been inching forward, stooping, tensed to the fluttering fraction of an instant when the magnetism would seize him and slam him against the barrier. One step. The next. The imperceptible whisk of air—and in one movement he had thrust himself with all his might, curled into a ball, and shot forward low on the ground.

His muscles wrenched and tore. He fought to keep his body compact, his strength enclosed. His limbs were pulled outward, tumult engaged him and blackness smashed inside his skull. Then he was skidding, face downward, gasping for air, flat out —and on the other side.

For the moment it took the pounding pain in his head to recede, he imagined an eternity. He imagined wild music, laughter and singing, storm and a great rushing. He imagined he hid his face from the pack hunting by and stopped his ears to the unearthly, alluring voice. He imagined—in a pause that existed nowhere and lasted forever—a delicate bare foot, whitened by moonlight, crossed by the thongs of a sandal; the toe pointing, deliberately touching his outflung hand where the salt crumbled over the palm and in the interstices of the fingers. And then the whisper of a laugh, drifting away into the night.

18

LUCY was curled in a dip in the ground between the trees, eyes glittering in a face pale among the shadows. He knelt down beside her. "Are you all right?"

"I think so," she said uncertainly.

He looked around. "What happened? You're alone. . . . Let me take you home."

"No . . ." Her voice had a soft insistence. "I want to stay here for a while. I'm all right. I just want to stay here for a little while longer. . . ." She touched his arm and he felt the fragile movement of her fingers.

"You're trembling, you're cold. Here . . ." He pulled off his sweater. She murmured, "No . . ." but he insisted, wrapping the sweater around her. She put herself into his arms and stayed there, curled into him, a downy weight, tremulous as a bird.

He maneuvered his left arm until he could read his watch. It had stopped. "I was a fat lot of good," he said bitterly. "What happened?"

"Nothing awful. Something . . . tremendous." She sought for words. "They put Mirabelle and Bunty in beautiful robes. There were some . . . prayers, I suppose, and singing. They danced round us; we waited. Then I had a—a vision, I think. You told me about her—remember? The queen who lives behind the north wind, the Mother of all living, the white goddess. You'll say I imagined it; you wouldn't have been able to see her."

The hairs prickled on the back of his neck. No—but he could almost believe he had heard her pass with her company of beasts, heard her siren's voice above the ghostly tumult. His arms tightened around Lucy. "It's one of the oldest legends, the wild hunt. And it would have happened at one time, the priestess riding out with her pack. It's part of a folk memory now, lodged in the unconscious. There could have been a time warp; there was a place for her in your mind, and she found it."

"Is that what happened? Yes, all right," Lucy said. He could not see her face but he could tell by the way her words sounded that she was smiling. His bitterness returned.

"I might as well not have been here. You didn't need me."

"You're wrong. I need you. Here, now . . . like this. I need you." She moved her head on his shoulder and whispered with her mouth close to his cheek.

He lifted her a little away. Her body was warm and yielding, heavy with the sensuous, boneless weight of a woman ready for love. He moved and she slid against him, pressing her thigh to him, seeking the statement of his desire, smiling as her softness encountered his hardness. "Lucy, if we stay here . . ."

"Yes. Here."

"If you're sure . . ." He was pulling her dress away; it slipped from her like water and her nakedness rose from it, luminous against the green-black shadows. There was no strangeness around them, only the quickening of the earth, the vivid need of the night. But he was careful of her because she was so vulnerable, and he had never treated any woman with selfishness or disrespect. "Darling, I haven't got anything. Does it matter?"

She shook her head, and waited as he dealt with his clothes, her hands touching him in small caresses, infinitely patient, that swelled and sped his blood beyond patience.

She had an extraordinary clinging persistence that made her plump little body powerful beneath his. She sought him as urgently as he sought her, opening her legs and pushing herself wetly and wildly against him; but when he entered her she lay as still as death and he paused and stroked her face and whispered, "Are you all right? You're so small, I don't want to hurt you."

She murmured, "You're not hurting," and he wondered if she lied, and wondered at the loving helplessness of women that drove them to give so much of themselves. He withdrew a little and she clutched at him convulsively, her eyes squeezed shut in her betrayed face. "No—"

"Ssh, there's no hurry. I'm not going to stop—"

She would not listen. Her hands were clenched into his back, her thighs enfolding his; with her fierce, passive persuasiveness she drove herself against him. He gasped, "Oh, Christ—" and then he could not stop.

They walked slowly back through the night, wrapped around each other. Lucy's head just reached his shoulder. "I should have been Bunty," she murmured.

"No. I wanted you to be you."

"Thank you." After a while she gave a low gurgle of laughter. "Bunty, *as well?*"

"Certainly not. After the age of forty, so the textbooks say, a man's sexual potency declines."

"Ah. We'll see about that," she said, and laughed again.

In the house she switched on lights carelessly. When Henry went to the curtains, she said, "No one can see us."

"Doesn't matter. Curtains are there to be drawn—my suburban upbringing. Whatever happened to yours?"

"God knows. I've a suspicion I'll find it again in the morning. Just now nothing matters. Shall we have coffee? Or would you like some wine?"

Her figure was reflected on the darkened pane, curled against the cushions of the sofa. Her voice reached him contentedly as he stood at the window.

"Who are your neighbors?"

"Field with horses on one side; on the other a vile house."

He had seen it, a stark red-brick square disciplined by conifers and geometric alternations of concrete and grass.

"He's an airline pilot. He looks like an indignant sheep, and he always seems to be incensed about something—garbage men or the taxes or the price of bacon. His wife's so faded she's scarcely *there.*"

"Have they lived here long?"

"Couple of years, I believe. We don't have much to do with them. We can't see them anyway, and they can't see us."

"No," he agreed, and drew the curtains against the night. The wood belonged to itself now and only owls hunted there; shadow and moonlight swathed the empty garden. *A secret place,* he thought, *such a secret place. Who knows who might come and go with no one to tell?*

They shared the sofa, comfortably, and drank wine. "Why did they just leave you there in the wood?" Henry asked.

"I don't know." Lucy had not thought about it. It occurred to her that as they had known of Henry's presence, they had known she would not be alone. She put up her hand and touched his face. This was not the time to calculate, or be sensible. If she had once again been used, it was for her own pleasure, and because a pattern was unfolding.

"Henry, do you believe they have powers out of the ordinary? Do you believe it now?"

"I believe they believe they have. That puts us all in the same state of mind."

"I'm sorry, that's a bit too complicated for me. There's nothing evil about them, I'm sure of that. If there's anything evil here, it's what's left over from that old magician."

"How? What do you mean?" Henry asked. He put down his wineglass and cuddled her. She leaned against him and began to tell him about the afternoon in the cellar, which led her to explain about Ruth Drake, and Ruth's interest in locating the part of the building that had been destroyed by fire; and then what had happened in that place the previous evening after the guests had gone.

"But why should I think of *you*, Henry?" she asked, rediscovering the least or perhaps the strangest thing in all that strangeness. "No. I didn't think. I wasn't *thinking*, not deliberately. It wasn't that you were in my mind; you were outside it, associated with . . . whatever it was. The awful sense of danger, of something going away, something terribly sad. You've never—no, you couldn't—you've never had anything to do with the magus, have you?"

"Not that I know of. I've never met him or spoken to him, if that's what you mean. I—"

"The book." She sat up suddenly, excitedly. "The book you had of his—*The Fifth Element.* Perhaps that was the connection."

"Rather a remote one," he murmured, his voice low because he had thought of something else; and if for an instant there were pain and anger in his eyes, the room was too softly lit for her to detect them.

"Still, it was something very personally his. . . . Secret, really. Er . . . esoteric?" She tried the word cautiously, looking at him for confirmation. He nodded encouragingly at her and she went on. "You were exposed to it, you read it—"

"I didn't understand it."

"Oh, neither did I. But maybe that doesn't matter."

"You know about it, though—what it was supposed to mean."

"Well, in a way," she said furtively. "I'm not supposed to talk about it."

"I can't see that it matters, between the two of us, can you?" he said reassuringly, and saw how every trace of guilt vanished from her face. He pulled her close again and kissed her and stroked the soft, suntanned arm that lay possessively across his chest. "Do you know who it was? Who did the ritual with him?"

"Who? . . . How do you mean?"

"There had to be someone, someone he called a disciple." He explained briefly, in the simplest terms. Once she had accepted the idea, she began to consider it aloud, testing herself against possibilities, rediscovering scraps of conversation she had overheard, at last murmuring, "No, no . . . How could I know? It was years ago, and they don't want to talk about it, except among themselves. I think they do that a lot. There's something they keep returning to, something they thought was over and done with; it must be that. I'll tell you what, Henry." Her hand sought his and gripped it fearfully. "Whoever it was, I sensed her there with him, in that awful emptiness, out there in the dark and the space."

Her. Lucy, not knowing what she was saying, said "her." Henry held her tightly, put his cheek against her silky hair and closed his eyes. After a moment, his hold on her relaxed. He said quietly, "Lucy, will you do something for me?"

"Yes, anything," she answered, a little wonderingly.

"Will you find out who it was?"

She sat up and studied him, bewilderment in her trusting brown eyes. "Why? Does it matter?"

"It's just that I want to know."

"I don't. Henry, if people do these weird things, it's for their own reasons; they *choose*, they *know*. We don't, we mustn't interfere. They take strange paths that lead to places we could never recognize. My God, am I really saying this? A few weeks ago I wouldn't even have been able to *think* it. . . ." She withdrew into her thoughts for a while, considering the unlikely transformation of herself. Then she gave up and slumped against him. "Henry, I'm *tired*."

He hugged her. "Let's go to bed, then."

"Yes."

"Will you try and find out for me?"

"All right. I'll probably make a mess of it, though. I'm not very good at being devious. I'm not very good at anything, really."

"Oh, yes you are," he said.
She giggled, and gave him a look almost as wicked as Bunty's.

Upstairs, she washed away the woody smell that occupied her body, left the bathroom light on and her dress lying on the floor like a drift of autumn leaves. She did not even glance at her own room but went into the big double room, pulled back the bedclothes, bundled Roland's pajamas and stowed them away out of sight.

She was aware of Henry moving about downstairs, washing the glasses, seeing that the doors and windows were locked. He was such a collected man, so controlled about everything; a nice, ordinary man with no blank, hazardous places in his life where he would be desperate for comfort. He didn't need her; he shared with her, respecting her sexuality. In the speeding moment when he lost himself and was her captive, he grudged her nothing. Because she knew he would be the same with any woman, she didn't feel guilty about him. There was something so unchallengeably *right* about what she was doing she couldn't even feel guilty about Roland. Or Bunty, who had first claim on Henry but had so mysteriously and deliberately relinquished it. And thinking of Bunty, it occurred to her to say to him, when he had tidily switched off the landing and bathroom lights and shut the door: "You know, Henry . . . if that book was so special, such a secret . . . why didn't she mind when I told her you'd lost it? You'd think she'd have a fit. But she didn't mind at all."

"She has her own reasons, I suppose," Henry murmured. The thieving little bitch.

"You've left the light on," Lucy said softly.

"I know. I want to see you."

"But I'm fat."

He laughed. "No, you're not. You're bonny."

"Do you like bonny women?"

He said, "Yes," and if it was not always true, it was true at that moment. Just as later, when he had switched off the lamp, he said,

"I love you," for with her softness and her giving, the wildness of her eyes and her nails digging into his back, it was almost true.

She was fast asleep, curled into a ball. He got out of bed carefully, without disturbing her, found his shoes and Roland's dressing gown and went quietly out of the room.

In Roland's study he went to the desk and swiftly, neatly, examined the contents of the drawers. When he came to one locked drawer, he thought at once of the key he had seen on the dressing table upstairs. Just one key. He went on thinking about it, weighing the chance and deciding it was worth a try. He moved softly in the bedroom, which was white with moonlight. The key made a faint scraping sound as he picked it up from the glass-topped dressing table. Lucy stirred, murmured and was still.

The key fitted the drawer, and in the drawer lay the black book. He opened it. The missing pages, the numbers of which he had memorized, were now in place, loosely inserted. He took them out, locked the drawer, put the key and the pages on the desk for his return and went out.

In the kitchen he picked up the flashlight he had earlier placed ready and went through the hall to where an inner door opened to the cellar—he had made sure the bolts were already drawn back. The door opened noiselessly inward. Silent as a cat, he went down into the dark, following the stab of light.

Lucy kissed him good-bye. Her cotton wrap was the color of cornflowers, crushing finely in his arms. He could feel her warm, sleepy body through the thin material. She put her hands against his chest, rested her head against him. "Thank you."

"For what?"

"Your body's so kind," she said, because in the night it had been. Now, under her hands, it was tense and impatient; something else, too. "Why are you sad?"

"I'm not," he lied.

"Yes. I can feel it. In here." She pressed her hands against him. "Whatever it is, I'm sorry."

"It's not you, or what we've done," he said.

"No." She stood back. "I was wrong about you. Something I thought: that there was nothing—no dark places in your life."

"We all have something."

"Yes, I suppose so." But she smiled, her warm, candid smile, and then nodded toward the French window, where the morning waited, vaporous, glimmering, shot through with dew. "Off you go," she said softly.

In the clearing between the garden and the trees he turned right to take the long way around. He would not go through the wood to the footbridge across the river; he needed to walk quickly in the silent beginning of the day till the house was far behind and the threads that held him to it had slackened.

He made plans, he glanced at his watch, he calculated the distance to Marleigh. And all the time, although he knew that in a physical sense he was alone, they stood at the very limits of his control: grave, mesmerized presences, stricken to their places in a mad dream that had died long ago.

. . . there's magic there . . . so I'm going . . . to the house and the trees . . . and the oblique ones. . . .

19

LUCY put down the telephone receiver. "Henry isn't there. He's still booked in, but he's gone off somewhere for the day. They expect him back later."

"I wonder where," Bunty murmured. She sat perched on the arm of one of the big chairs, her body all angles and tension. She looked unhappy. Mirabelle sat across the room, sketching her; she had an absorbed calm, as if she was guarding herself against an invisible enemy.

Lucy remembered the day she had met Ruth Drake, the sunlit day when she had the sensation that everything was falling to pieces around her. It felt like that again now; it was awful. Not even the recollection of Henry could comfort her. The peaceful early morning had ticked slowly away toward a half-realized suspense. Then Bunty had arrived, pedaling up the driveway at the front of the house, wheels skidding as she wrenched her bicycle to a halt. With delayed surprise, Lucy now pondered the fact: *I actually saw her arrive.* Had Bunty lost her uncanny facility for materializing out of thin air? Was she different?

Or am I different?

She went to the window to look out onto the beautiful tangle of Mirabelle's garden. Mirabelle's house, next door to Bunty's, was furnished, like Bunty's, in an elegant, faded way, everything old-fashioned and comfortable. Except the paintings. Lucy did not look at them; they made her nervous.

"Your garden, these houses . . . everything's so shut in." She didn't say claustrophobic, but it was what she felt. She longed for the space of her own house, the open lawns, the spreading shrubbery.

"Light," Mirabelle said.

"Sorry." Lucy moved away from the window. She looked over her shoulder at Roland. "You might have told me," she said accusingly for the third or fourth time; she had lost count. "I don't see why you couldn't have told me you were here last night. Any of you."

"Would it have made any difference?" Mirabelle murmured.

"He shouldn't have been anyway," Bunty said.

"I didn't want to be too far away from you, Lucy," Roland said, at last giving her a direct answer. Lucy overlooked it; she was wondering if it *would* have made any difference. She had an unreal, unregretted feeling about making love with Henry, and a shameless conviction that he'd only have to ask her and she'd do it again without a minute's thought. She wondered if Roland knew. Bunty and Mirabelle wouldn't tell him, she was certain of that, just as she was certain *they* knew; they knew everything. Except where Henry was. Did it matter?

"What does it matter?" she asked of no one in particular. "What does it matter where Henry is, or who he is? Why do you want to know?"

"Because we don't," Bunty said, with impatient logic, looking at Mirabelle, who smiled and murmured, "Don't fidget, doll."

Bunty sighed and was still.

Mirabelle said, "Make some tea, Roland." Instead of answering, *Make it yourself, it's your house,* he got up to do it. Lucy said quickly, "He *drops* things. I'll do it."

She went into the kitchen and he followed her, helping her to find her way about the shelves and cupboards. "If you wanted to be near me, and you knew I was in the wood, you could have come *there,*" she said.

"No, I couldn't. That was no place for me last night. I would have interfered with their magic."

"I thought you hated it."

"Some things are necessary."

She had been about to say, *A man* was *there.* What stopped her was not a desire to protect herself but a desire to save Roland from any further admission of failure. So tied by his own conflict, so damaged by it, he *had* no place in that sensuous revel; he would have represented destruction, blasphemy. Worse, he would have been ludicrous. But Henry, Henry came cleanly from outside with no loyalties or regrets, only a need unashamedly wakened that recognized and answered hers.

She looked at Roland. She thought he seemed almost defeated; but there was a calmness about him, as if he had accepted something that had given him completeness. She said, "You're a real person. For the first time you're a real person." She had an impulse to touch him to prove this to herself, and to him, but instead she became busy setting out cups and saucers on a tray. She felt that he was studying her and turned her head, shaking back her tumbled brown hair.

He said quietly, "You do realize you're wearing scarcely any clothes. You look almost disgraceful."

"I must," she agreed with a puzzled awareness that, for once, he was not trying to make her feel ashamed of herself. Her cotton jeans were one size too small, her blue cotton shirt skimpy and sleeveless. She had forgotten or had not cared to put on any underwear. Straining seams everywhere advertised the curves of her plump little body.

"You look like a cornfield," he said. "Like a cornfield in the sun." He touched the soft swell of her breast, caressing her gently, reassuringly; then he put his arms around her and held her for a moment. "Strong little Lucy."

"Strong? Me?"

"Yes. More than you know."

From the other room Bunty's high-pitched voice called, "That's enough of that. Tea."

Lucy gave an explosive giggle. "My God, she must have ears like a bat. She can hear the kettle boiling from in there."

"I can hear something boiling," Bunty wailed.

Lucy, busy with the teapot, spoke softly. "Roland, what's going to happen?"

He didn't answer at once. He spilled milk filling the jug for her, dropped a spoon. "Lucy, I love you. I need you."

"I know. That's why you married me."

"Think of that, whatever happens. Think of that."

Lucy tipped her handbag onto the cushions of the sofa, searching for cigarettes. An envelope fell out. It was heavily scented, the miniature, flourished handwriting adamant on its lilac surface. Bunty picked it up disbelievingly. "It looks like a letter from a brothel."

"My mother," Lucy said, reclaiming it.

"Gawd," Bunty murmured.

Mirabelle, passing, balancing her cup and saucer, observed, "You haven't opened it."

"I don't need to." The contents were so predictable Lucy could have recited them. The gossip might vary in detail but its mind-stunning triviality remained constant. The demands to be invited for a visit were becoming increasingly shrill, the speculations on Lucy's sex life increasingly offensive. "I don't like her letters much."

"I don't think you like her much," Mirabelle said.

Lucy pondered this. "No. I never have, really."

Bunty was curious. "Can I read it?"

"If you want to." Lucy put her hand protectively on Roland's knee and smiled at him. She was too much at home with them, with their knowledge of her, to feel any embarrassment.

Bunty read the first page. "Prurient cow. What business is it of hers how often Roland does you; or how? Or doesn't, as it happens. Her euphemisms are more indecent than my language."

"Impossible," Mirabelle murmured.

"True. Oh, God. Listen. 'As you refuse to tell me what precautions you're taking, I can only assume you're on the pill. I'm *very*' —underlined twice—'upset about this. I ought to be kept fully informed about the risks you're taking because you realize you can drop down dead of a thrombosis at any minute and how would I face the neighbors?' "

"She's not real," Mirabelle said.

"She bloody is. Lucy . . ."

Lucy had scarcely been listening. She was smiling at Roland, who smiled back at her and murmured, "There you are. Strong. You survived your upbringing."

"Only just. And you."

He looked wretched. Lucy said with quiet insistence, "*Yes, yes.*"

"Lucy," Bunty said. "We don't want her here. Ever."

"You keep her away, then," Lucy answered equably.

"Oh, we will. Mirabelle will. Something moderate but effective. Now, Father . . ." Bunty's tone became provocative. She gave Roland a wicked look. "Father would have done something much too dramatic. Caused a sending, probably."

"A what?" Lucy asked.

"An elemental," Roland explained. "A demon to torment her."

"I bet it would have rebounded," Bunty said.

Lucy could not let the opportunity pass; it was almost as if she had been presented with a cue. She made hesitant, rather wandering comments about Roland's father and his magic, working around to her point. Eventually, she said, "That last time . . . the important thing . . . the last ceremony . . ."

They were watching her, sitting in absorbed silence. No one prompted her, no one did anything except wait; but Lucy, concentrating hard, didn't notice this.

". . . There was somebody with him. Didn't you tell me, Roland? Or was it you, Bunty? Someone did, anyway. Who was it?"

She was conscious of her words resting on the unmoving air, of the sunless, stifling day, the faces regarding her. *No, I don't want to know,* she thought, but she couldn't say it. Her mind splintered on images that seemingly had no connection: the ridiculous, inconclusive errand to Henry at The Feathers; the door between the hall and the dining room standing open after her telephone call to him; his presence in the wood; the key of the desk—which Roland always kept on his key ring—lying on the dressing table.

Bunty made a distracted movement, running her hand through her short chestnut hair. She looked at Roland with panic, or appeal, on her face. "Nobody. Tell her there was nobody."

But Roland didn't answer; he turned his head from Lucy, receiving Bunty's wild glance. Lucy had kept her hand upon his knee; through her fingers, her palm, she felt his stillness, his completeness. Mirabelle stood up and went with her languorous, sweeping stride to Bunty. She stood beside her, smoothing the ruffled curls. Then she looked at Roland with her opaque, lightless eyes, and Lucy was afraid.

20

THE note to Henry read:

Meet me at the fort this evening. I'll wait from eight o'clock. Please, it's important,

Lucy

P.S. I know who it was.

The fort was deserted. The gauze of cloud that had hung in the sky had parted toward evening and now the sun glinted between the trees, dazzling the moving leaves. Henry walked the circumference of the rampart, then went down into the silent scoop of the hollow and stood, undecided, in the center. After a moment, something made him turn and look up.

Bunty stood on the rampart, a fragile figurine outlined by the gilt of the setting sun. He ran up the slope, as if he expected her to vanish before he reached her. But she was real enough, very small as he stood over her, looking up at him with her melancholy eyes. He said, "You sent me that note. Lucy might have written it but you sent it." He remembered Bunty's handwriting, the large, decisive letters on the sheet of paper in her workroom.

"Would you have come if I'd asked you? You don't trust me."

"Can you blame me," he said bitterly. "Why here?"

She gave a slight shrug. "Neutral ground."

"Neutral ground. There's no such thing round here. Every inch of it belongs to your kind; it has for centuries."

"I didn't expect you to understand that."

"I know. And you didn't expect me to resist that first spell, that night at your house. You didn't expect me to fight back."

"That's true. You were terribly strong. I touched something primitive in you."

"You recognized it, of course," he said, with faint irony.

"Of course," she repeated, in the same tone.

They stood in silence. A breeze stirred from tree to tree, whispering across the sacred clearing. Henry, feeling how patiently the dead waited to occupy the dark, thought, *I wouldn't care to be here at night.*

"We've all been here," Bunty said. "This is where we began: you, me, everyone. We've shouted and sung and smelled the blood of sacrifice."

"But you believe in reincarnation."

"Yes." She didn't ask him what he believed in. "Shall we walk?"

They went along the rampart and down, away from the deserted place, returning together along the track Henry had walked earlier alone.

"I was supposed to wake up later, in your bed, perhaps. And never know you'd left me, to steal your father's book."

"Did I steal it?" she said, amusing herself by pretending to gasp at her own daring.

"And then what? A love affair to divert me. To give you the opportunity to find out if I was here quite innocently. That was what you wanted."

"I want," Bunty said, deliberately changing the tense, "I want you to be here innocently. I want to divert you. I could."

"You're wrong. You've run out of time, little elf."

Her plaintive voice held a wild note. "There was something about you right from the start. There you were, so casual, so sexy, and all the time some damn bloody festering determination, lurking under the surface. You didn't do what I wanted, what I expected. You didn't do anything, you just—oh, you just went on being you, half out of reach; being determined. It made me afraid."

"Not of me. Of something inside yourself; something you are —or know."

"There, you see . . . lurking." There was a strain in her manner, and he noticed how careful she had been to say "I" and not "we."

They had reached the stile. Henry went over first and turned to help her, looking at her long skirt. "Can you manage?"

"Oh, yes." And she did, without any fuss or fumbling, stepping up lightly and pausing at the top. Between the thongs of her sandals her bare feet were powdered with dust from the track; beneath the slightly lifted hem of her skirt her ankles were delicate and tense as a thoroughbred's. She sprang, a reckless movement to which he responded instinctively, putting his arms out to catch her.

She stood a little away from him as he grasped her, her hands reaching up to rest on his shoulders. She smiled, but her eyes were somber. "I did want you, Henry. Very much. I didn't want to keep away from you, but I had to. You were dangerous."

"To you, maybe. Not to Lucy."

She turned from him and they went on down the track. "Lucy needed you. You must ask her why. I think you ought to know."

He didn't respond to this for fear bitterness might betray him. Of all the things he needed to know, one was not—not yet—confirmation of the buried suspicion that there was nothing accidental about what had happened with Lucy. He had planned to use her, it was true, in any way that suited his purpose; but had she used him? Or were they both pawns in someone else's game?

"Part of the design," Bunty said. He had sensed how she was keyed up, her nerves exposed, a state that obviously facilitated her uncanny ability to pick up his thoughts.

He said, "And Smith. Was she part of the design?"

Bunty made a slight movement of her shoulders, as if gathering herself together. "Smith? I don't know about her."

He caught her arm and swung her around. She winced, not because he was hurting her but because the pitch and intensity of his voice cut through her defenses. "Oh, yes you do."

She drew away from him, carefully. "If I tell you what I know, will you go away?"

"It depends what you tell me."

There was some objection she wanted to make to this, but from the way she looked at him he could tell she didn't dare.

"It was a long time ago. Smith was just someone who drifted here and then drifted away again."

"Really? Of her own volition? In both directions?"

"Of course. Direction had nothing to do with her; she was like that."

He didn't need anyone to tell him what Smith was like. "And where did she drift to?"

"Gosh, how should I know?" Bunty said, lying too skillfully. "I don't even know where she drifted from. She said she had no one: no family, no ties, nothing. If you want to find her, you'll have to go looking somewhere else. She didn't leave an address, or any messages."

"I've looked somewhere else. I've looked everywhere else. I've been to every single place and person that was remotely connected with her. It's taken me a long time, and I've covered the ground too thoroughly to make any mistakes. You know where she came from, all right: you, Roland, Mirabelle and your father met her in Marleigh in the garden of Mrs. Jane Cartwright. She left with you that same evening and was later seen in your company. When the Festival was over, you all returned here and she accompanied you. Since then, nobody has seen her, nobody has heard from her. Nobody. Now. Where did she go?"

Bunty halted in her quick stride. She looked straight at him, the dense gold of the evening sun full on her face. In her eyes there was an anxiety she could not hide, but she said firmly and steadily, "I don't know. I swear to you, on my honor, that I don't know where Smith is."

For a moment he studied her face, then despairingly blanked it out as he looked inward at his own anguish. He knew she was telling the truth.

Bunty took his hand gently. "Who was she, Henry?"

"My sister."

"Oh . . ." Blankness closed stealthily over her expression.

They resumed their walk. Before them the tower of the church rose, mellow in the evening light.

"My half sister," Henry said. "I think. We were never sure. We had the same mother, but it was never any good asking her because she couldn't be certain about anything. Our parents were divorced when we were very young. I stayed with my father; he never married again. My mother did, though; twice. That's not counting other men she set up house with. Smith lived with her sometimes, sometimes with us. She coped quite happily with all the upheavals. The only thing she found really difficult was the constant change of surname."

"So she called herself Smith."

"It made things easier."

"It made her anonymous. She said that. She also said she'd mislaid her identity very early in life but it didn't matter. . . . I can see now what she must have meant. She told whopping lies and never expected you to believe them; she was crazy, a clown." Bunty's high voice scaled toward laughter at something remembered, then she checked herself, turning a searching and impersonal glance on him. "Not a bit like you. Not a bit—that way. But the first time I met you I thought I'd seen you before. There's a likeness, very faint . . . gone when you look for it."

"Why did she come here with you?" Henry asked.

"Why did she go anywhere with anyone?"

"Because she had to commit herself to people, ideas. She had to assume personalities, states of being. It was a compulsion with her. The more bizarre, the more inexplicable, the more likely she would be to solve the enigma of her identity—or find someone to solve it for her. . . ." And these elusive people, touched by glamour, forever striving against each other and yet strangely coherent—their magic would be irresistible to her.

Bunty glanced uneasily up at him. "You understood her very well, considering you're so different. Is that what she was running away from? Your common sense? Your stolidity?"

"Why running away? Motion implies direction—"

"But not necessarily a destination. That's something you'd find hard to grasp and she would know without even thinking. And she did tell us"—unheedingly cruel, Bunty went on—"she did tell us she had no one, quite deliberately."

"All her lies were deliberate."

"Thank you," Bunty said sharply. "You've just proved my argument."

They were walking beside the low church wall. Bunty sat down on it, took off her sandal and extracted some grass that had worked between the thongs. Henry sat beside her, watching her. When she made to rise, he took her wrist and held her still. Her small face became stealthy once more; she wouldn't meet his eyes. The silence between them strained to the point where she was forced to break it.

"*Leave* her, Henry. She wanted to be left alone; that's why she *was* alone."

"She was with you."

"Not for long. A few days."

"At your father's house."

"Yes. Then she went away."

"When?"

"I don't know. I don't remember. Just afterwards, it was a bad time: there was that accident and the fire in Father's laboratory . . . then Father died . . . then Roland was ill."

"Your father died in a nursing home a fortnight after returning from Marleigh."

"Yes."

"Why was Roland ill?"

"Not ill physically. He had a nervous collapse." She gave a sardonic little laugh. "The accumulated strain of family life; years of personality collisions. He was always the weakest. When Father died, things fell apart, especially Roland."

"Yes . . ." Henry murmured, remembering how Bartholomew Thwaite had said: *their conflicts would be internal, and consuming.* . . . "So Smith just stayed for a few days, then left."

"Yes. I told you. Well, there's nothing remarkable in that. It's the sort of thing people—"

"Did you see her go?"

Bunty faltered. "What? Well, no. Not *see* her . . ."

"Did Roland, or Mirabelle?"

"I don't know. I suppose so."

"Then I'll ask them."

"It won't do any *good.* She was here, she went away, I've told you. It's what you wanted to know. That's all there is."

"No."

She looked away. He still held her wrist, fine-boned as a bird's, in his hand. "Who sent you to tell me this? Mirabelle?"

"Roland," she said, her head tilted away from his disbelieving look. "Aren't you satisfied now? There's nothing else anyone can tell you."

"The fifth element?"

The sharpened movement of her body betrayed a sudden increase in tension, but she said, "Oh, that . . ." in a dismissing voice.

"That."

"There was nothing special about it. My father had been performing magic rituals all his life. . . ."

"Not that one. That was the last. He needed Smith for it. He used her."

"Well, all right." Bunty gave a sigh and then began to speak swiftly. "But that's the way these things work; you wouldn't understand. That's why we took him to Marleigh—he knew he would find the embodiment of his spirit there. And she had to be in the garden that night; it was her time and her hour, too. Poor Smith, she'd searched all her life for the completeness of her life. Some people have that yearning for their destiny; they don't know when it will come to them, what form it will take, what it will do to them; but when it happens they're ready, they know. There was no question of persuasion—it was simply a matter of recognition."

Bunty was clever; but she couldn't possibly be clever enough to know how he was forced to admit Smith's own estimation of herself in these fantastic, self-deluded terms.

"Did she know what he wanted?"

"Oh, yes. It was what she wanted, too. But we had to be sure. Roland had to come back here for a couple of days and he brought her with him. That was when he gave her the book. And we thought—Mirabelle thought—that away from Father's influence for a little while, she might see things differently, she might change her mind. But she didn't. She never even read the book, not then. As soon as she got back to Marleigh, she asked Father if she should. Actually, we didn't know that, till afterwards, till it was all over."

"He said yes, but he removed certain pages before he gave it back to her."

Bunty nodded and stirred uneasily. "Henry, let go of my wrist. Let's walk back to the hotel."

They went between the churchyard yews and out into the curving, cobbled streets. The last of the sun had gone but the air was still stiflingly warm. He watched Bunty and saw that she crossed her arms once or twice as if to clutch at a shiver on her skin.

Eventually—she explained—they had all returned to Nine Maidens. There were two days of preparation, then the ceremony itself. Henry asked where and she answered, "In the house, of course."

"Yes. But where?"

"He had a sort of laboratory—I told you, the one that was destroyed. It was built onto the side of the house. He'd once done alchemical experiments there—and some rites; it was purified."

"And the cellar?"

"Yes, there, too. That was the inner temple; the second part of the ceremony was carried out there."

"Did any of you assist?"

"Oh, no." The idea seemed to surprise her. "It wasn't necessary. And they had to be closed off. Any disruptive influences would have weakened the force." She spoke in a matter-of-fact way, and yet there was a tinge of irony to her tone, as if she knew and pitied other people's delusions. "But it's no good asking me any more, Henry. I don't know. I wasn't there."

"What?" He looked at her sharply.

"No. I had to go to London—if you don't believe me, you can check up on me. I was away two days. When I came back, it was over, and she'd gone."

He swore in exasperation, and then walked for a while in silence. Bunty murmured, "I'm sorry," then she fell silent, too.

As they entered the square, the luminous blue twilight was stealing into the sky. They faced each other. Bunty said, "Will you go away now, Henry?"

"No. I haven't finished, have I?"

"Please go," she urged softly. "You won't find her here. I don't think you'll find her anywhere. She was changed, after that. She became what she wanted to be. Don't you understand? She searched, and she found. She isn't the Smith you know anymore."

"Who told you that?"

"Mirabelle."

"Do you believe her?"

"Of course." Her trust in Mirabelle was so absolute she seemed faintly surprised that anyone should question it. "She's my blood, my faith, everything. I would do whatever she said, believe whatever she said."

"Even if, in your heart, you knew it wasn't true?"

"It has to be. . . ." Suddenly, in the melancholy of her eyes, there was a desperate appeal.

"We must find out. Come along." He led her toward his car.

21

SHE said they must drive to her house because Mirabelle would be there. Henry considered this for a moment and then shrugged. It sounded almost a condition of surrender. As they twisted through the high-banked lanes where the trees made tunnels and wild honeysuckle wreathed, he thought: one thing—in such a haunted landscape they would never lack a stage setting for their deceptions.

Then, when they reached Bunty's house, Mirabelle was not there—as Bunty pointed out, unnecessarily and apologetically.

"Really?" Henry said, standing in the open doorway.

At the dry note in his voice she spread her hands and gave a little shrug, perhaps of acceptance, but the hallway was too dim for him to see clearly and she had not switched on the light. "I know where we'll find her, though. We'll go through the wood."

"Very well. But if you'll let me use your telephone, it won't take a moment."

"Of course." She switched on the light and stood across the hall from him, watching him guardedly as he went to the telephone. When he had dialed, and the number answered, he said, "Henry Beaumont . . . Yes . . . Yes, I'm sure. . . . At the time, that will do."

As he had said, it took only a moment; but surprise quickened on her face when he put down the receiver after those few words and went to the door, turning to wait for her. She went close to him and, seeing he would tell her nothing, shrugged away her curiosity; she was occupied by matters important to her, to them both. She looked into his face. "You're not afraid of the wood anymore."

"I was never afraid."

"No . . . But last time you brought salt, as a protection against evil. There's no evil there. Justice, perhaps, completeness, realization."

"What a lot of nonsense you talk," he said quietly.

"Maybe. Not all of it's nonsense, though, and you know it. At least you were some way towards understanding, at least you showed respect. That was why you could break into the circle. Oh, you might not admit now that there are two worlds, but you did then. You *knew*—and for a little while you were between them."

The day had died to a soft, engrossing dusk; the great, shrouded heads of the trees were motionless and the river trembled, half green, half dark. Bunty walked so lightly in her thin sandals the only sound was the sound of Henry's footsteps on the wooden boards of the bridge. They went without speaking—only a few steps, it seemed to him, but when he turned to look back, the trees had closed behind them and the lights that had glimmered in the houses beyond the river were lost to view.

Bunty's hand rested on his arm. He felt the suppleness of her movements, her warm, weightless presence, and heard the whispering *swish-swish* of her long skirt.

"Why is it there's never anyone in this wood?" he asked.

"But there is," she answered. "There."

A little way ahead, where the path widened, a woman waited. Her long, pale dress blurred against the darkening background and even in repose her slender body had Bunty's grace; but she was tall, almost tall enough to match Henry's height. She put out her hand in a slight, subtle gesture of welcome and Bunty, who had left him and gone swiftly to her, took her hand and said, "Mirabelle, Smith was his sister."

"I see."

Henry could read no change of expression in the calm, high-cheekboned face, the strange, pale eyes. Her voice had a light, faintly languid music to its tone, soft and very clear.

"Bunty's told you what she can. You don't believe her."

"How do you know that?"

"Because you're here." Again she made the beautiful, eloquent gesture, inviting him to walk while she walked beside him. Like a small shadow, Bunty accompanied them; perhaps sometimes she walked behind them and Henry felt he should keep her in sight, but in spite of himself his attention was drawn irresistibly to Mirabelle.

"Will you believe me?" she asked.

"Not if you tell me the same things."

"I don't know any more."

"There *is* more."

"Is there? Don't you know already what you really came to find out?"

Now her hand, with the very faintest pressure, rested on his arm. The words Bunty had spoken earlier found an echo in his mind—or perhaps she, or Mirabelle, repeated them in that drifting, dark green, entranced place: *She became what she wanted to be. . . . She searched . . . she found. . . .*

With an effort he resisted the words and all the implications they contained, pushing them beyond the boundary of his will until they became meaningless, entangled in the scorn, the impatience he felt for these women, their fantasies, their deceptions.

"In that case," Mirabelle said, "we must all be convinced."

He had an impulse to shake off the hand that held him by its light, caressing touch, but even in his anger he knew this would be the rudest return of the courtesy she was offering. Instead, he said almost diffidently, "Damn you and your tricks."

"Telepathy isn't a trick. It's a gift. One can cultivate it."

"One might. I can't. I'm too earthbound. Your web's too intricate to contain any but your own kind. I've just blundered in looking for answers to questions, and I won't go until I get them."

"Oh, we knew you'd come. One day," Mirabelle said.

"Precognition? Or simple common sense? If a woman disappears, someone's bound to come looking for her eventually."

"But to trace *her*, someone so elusive . . . And you, we weren't sure about you at all. You have what Bunty calls a lurking quality; it made you difficult to deal with. Still, we thought we might turn you back."

"Are you admitting defeat?"

"I'm admitting nothing." Her face, calm with its secrets, turned to his. "And then last night you took some pages from the book in Roland's desk. How clever of you. But what good can they do you? You can't understand them."

How clever of you. The merest flick of insolence in her voice was all that was necessary to open the reluctant doors in his mind, showing himself to himself so cunningly, so inevitably drawn on: from Lucy's telephone call (which they had known she would—and allowed her to—make); his presence in the wood, in the house; the key left for him to find.

Why? Because, proud and enclosed as they were, there was a secret they could no longer bear to support. He had discovered nothing and they had revealed nothing; it was simply that he was the instrument of an unbidden desire for discovery, justice, expiation.

They had entered a deserted clearing, where they paused. Henry said, "No, I couldn't understand, but I went to someone who could. A man called Bartholomew Thwaite."

Mirabelle answered softly, "I know of him. Yes. I see."

"It was plain then," Henry said, unaware that his voice had hardened to an almost businesslike tone. "In spite of the esoteric terms and the clotted prose: the disciple had to be prepared to die."

Bunty gave a small cry that trembled despairingly in the stillness. She looked fearfully from Mirabelle to Henry. "No, but she didn't. His magic wasn't strong enough for that—to take her life. . . ."

"His magic," Henry said derisively. "That was a hell of a price for an old man's vanity."

Bunty cried, "It's not true—it didn't happen. Mirabelle, it *didn't*. . . ."

Mirabelle had released Henry. She pressed her long, slim

hands together, dipping her head so that her hair drifted forward. "He was extremely destructive, in his life, in his death—you know that, Bunty."

"And you know what happened," Henry said. "Bunty only suspects, she's half suspected it for a long time. She's pushed it to the back of her mind and blindly gone on believing whatever you've told her to believe. But you know. You were here."

"No. Roland was here. . . ."

Henry had been sure the clearing was deserted; but perhaps the thickets, the shadows, the stately, rearing trees had deceived him—because he looked and saw Lucy was there, standing to one side, quite close, standing very still, with a restful composure. He went to her and kissed her cool mouth. In what was left of the light he could read a certain strain in her expression, a strain like the aftermath of shock.

"What's happened?" he asked.

Her attention went beyond him, to Mirabelle and Bunty; or something else. Her hand closed on his with purpose and she moved toward the center of the clearing, drawing him with her. "There's something you want to know . . . something none of us know. But if we wait, if we stand here . . ."

He saw that Mirabelle was walking without haste, gliding soundlessly over the cushiony moss. Bunty, standing to his left, pivoted her body slowly, following Mirabelle's movements, until Mirabelle made a sinuous inward turn to where they were standing.

"Here, in the circle," Lucy said.

Where Mirabelle had walked there was now a white circle surrounding them all; it was mysteriously luminous and trembling faintly, as if it had risen from the ground beneath her feet. Henry wrenched his gaze from it. "Lucy, for God's sake, what have you got to do with this idiotic charade?"

"No, please." She looked up at him with urgent yet self-contained appeal. "Please, because I ask you. Just wait. That's all."

"The circle isn't to imprison you," Mirabelle said politely. "It is, rather, a demarcation: the limit—if you wish—of our power. It does have protective properties, but you will be quite safe if you wish to step outside. It's better, though, if you remain here."

The moment she stopped speaking, all sound drained away. As he stared at her, Henry was aware that his senses had opened out and that he stood at the very heart of an uncanny stillness. He could not believe that the pressure of air held him motionless, that absolute peace had entered him; but these had happened, down in the depths of his being where everything had ceased to strive, where he was completely himself, if only for an instant.

There was a flicker of light, something that flashed beyond the circle. He never knew, even afterward, what caused it; he only knew that then he turned his attention to it with a reluctance as desolate as if his spirit groaned: *Go away, leave me in peace* . . . and a shape moved, vast, indistinguishable, beyond the trees.

"Aleph . . ."

Somebody whispered. Somebody whispered a mocking summons that, piercing, challenging, turned Henry's blood to ice.

"Aleph . . . Aleph . . ."

He had a violent impulse to snatch at the women and hold them. He never knew how he controlled it, but he was eternally thankful that he had. His desire to protect them was not merely misplaced, it was futile; the arrogant, waiting poise of their bodies told him that. And it was they—Mirabelle, or Bunty, or even Lucy—who summoned the magus from his lair. Although Lucy trembled a little, and Bunty's face had a blank, inward look, still they held to their certainty in themselves: nothing could move them or reduce their pride.

Mirabelle's voice held a scorn so pure it seemed to cut cleanly into the darkness. "Well, Aleph, what have you had to comfort you on your cosmic wanderings? Hatred? Indignity? The hatred you left in Roland, the indignity you left for Lucy. Is that what you need to sustain your vengeful soul?"

The ground must rise out there, Henry thought, giving an illusion of height. For it was an illusion: whatever the circle might contain, out beyond it was the trickery, the sham, the broken-stringed puppet in his trashy robes. This was no audacious masquerade nudging the unwilling mind toward the edge of doubt; this was the inept and vulgar mimicry that invited catcalls. If Henry had laughed aloud it would have been a very bitter laugh; but he was silent, and what held him still was his contempt.

The voice that came from behind the hood was unsexed, shrill and thin. "I found my way back," it piped. "I found my way back through her." The draperies rippled and the long arm pointed at Lucy.

"Why? Why her?" Bunty flung at him defiantly.

The arm wavered. "Because I *chose.*"

Henry cursed impatiently under his breath. "He's forgetting his lines, or you're not feeding the right cues. This is—"

"*Don't,*" Bunty said. She clung to his arm and he felt the drag of her weight as he would never have dreamed he would feel it, heavy and despairing.

"Don't you realize this is a fake?" he said.

"We have to let him try—this last time. We've opened all the ways, we've opened the wood—ourselves. This once he might come—in Roland. . . ." She turned her face from him. Her voice wailed across the clearing, "Did Smith give her spirit to you? Or did you take it?"

There was an utter silence. The magus stepped forward into a pool of moonlight. He lifted his hand and touched his brow, his chest, his right shoulder, his left shoulder, making the sign of the equal-armed cross that signified the four elements and the four cardinal points; with that he cast himself upon his magic, and from his betrayed universe his voice howled unendurably in the recesses of Henry's skull: *I failed. I took her life.*

Henry heard a cry, something blurred and unplaceable. His rage had at last smashed inside him and he hurled himself toward the robed figure that appeared, in a moment of blood-red confusion, to be receding. As he grasped it and tore off the hood, it shrank in his hands; it was all too solid flesh and bone, but limp, unresisting. In disgust he thrust it from him and it sagged to the ground.

For Christ's sake don't let me kick him while he's lying there. It was not that he had not done such a thing before; but what he feared, now that his patience had come to an end, was that his control would fail with it and the anguish he had tried so hard to hold at bay would at last possess him.

"Wake up. Get up, Roland," he said, grim with contempt.

Then he looked up, and saw stupidly that the women had not moved, that there was no circle, no clearing, just a very small space in the trees where they had all been standing. Lucy, between Bunty and Mirabelle, was staring at him from a deathly pale face, and he realized that the cry he had heard had been from her.

He went to her and took her cold, outstretched hand. It seemed that the women on either side touched him softly, tenderly, because they knew he was suddenly afraid and did not want to admit that something outside the world he knew and understood had, for a fraction of time, existed and found expression.

Lucy said, "She was thinking of you. The moment that she died, she was thinking of you. I have to tell you that."

22

LUCY sat beside Roland, holding his hand. Even in the shaded lights of the sitting room, Henry's face had such a harsh look she thought she would wait a little before she asked him if Roland would be taken to spend the night in the police station. She occupied herself with practical considerations. It would, she thought, be rather like someone going to a hospital. She must see he had his shaving kit, his pajamas, his dressing gown, his slippers.

"Do you feel better?" she asked quietly.

"Yes. Fine," Roland said.

Bunty was sitting opposite them in an armchair, her feet tucked into her long skirt, her arms hugging her knees. She studied Roland broodingly. "What was it like?"

"Fire," he answered. "Then nothing. Just nothing. I remember beginning to make the sign . . . then I don't remember anything else, until I came round."

Lucy suppressed a shudder. It seemed to her that in housing the spirit of the magus—even for a mere second of measurable time—he had endured immeasurable corruption; yet he had survived. . . . *So have I,* she thought. But what she had experienced as she stood inside the circle had been instantaneous, something self-annihilating that flared and fled and left only the faintest impress of itself, remote as a misplaced memory. Which was what it had been, a memory not her own, using her mind, occupying it for the purpose of reenacting the final, convulsive moment of an insane battle: the old man, exhausted by his unavailing sorcery, proffering the ceremonial cup; and the woman, smiling mysteriously from the shadow of her hood, taking, drinking, knowing. . . . Yes; knowing.

Roland squeezed her hand, saying to her, "It's all over now."

Henry looked at them, at the way they sat together; then at Mirabelle, who was poised on the arm of Bunty's chair. He threw his half-smoked cigarette into the empty fireplace, a gesture of exasperation, although his voice was even. "You're all taking this very calmly."

"Breeding," Mirabelle murmured.

"Even Lucy?"

"Why not?" Bunty said, as if she resented this singling out of one of their number. She muttered, as if to herself, "No one who calls me a posh tart can be all bad."

"What choice do we have anyway?" Mirabelle said. "You'd already arranged things."

Henry looked toward the opened windows, where the curtains hung unmoving, framing the distant darkened mass of the wood. "You did a bit of that yourself."

"It had to be done. For Roland's sake. Everybody's, really."

"What has Henry arranged?" Lucy asked timidly.

"A search warrant, or whatever the officialese is. To open the inner temple in the cellar."

"Oh . . . yes. But you don't mean *before.* Earlier. How could you? You didn't know—until someone told you in the wood." Someone. Mirabelle? Roland? Lucy had rather lost track of things, and it showed.

Bunty said, "He took a chance. Supposing you'd made a mistake, though. What then?"

"I could have called it off. . . ."

Long ago—centuries ago—Lucy had taken a shock that had splintered her to pieces. But then, out of her everlasting, incredible durability, she had put herself together again, and before the process had quite finished she had accepted the knowledge that the body of that poor, unknown woman was sealed away down there. She felt a distant, untraceable ache inside herself: for the woman, for Henry, for Roland.

What she still found unbelievable was that Roland—Roland had arranged and managed everything himself. Roland said, "The experiment was a failure, but Smith wasn't to know that. Only my father knew. He'd always been accustomed to handling strange, dangerous substances—drugs, distillations of plants—using them to assist an exaltation of consciousness. When at last he realized his magic couldn't draw her spirit from her . . . he gave her hemlock. And she took it . . . not knowing." For a moment his eyes sought Lucy's. She gazed back at him without a word and he went on. "He left her there. He told me it was necessary for her to remain, alone, in a consecrated place until . . . oh, I forget. He had some reason. He was near collapse, he was old and ill, the strain—the intensity of all those hours . . . I couldn't make much sense of it, and I was concerned—"

"Not about her, it seems," Henry said coldly.

"Good God, she was young and strong. She'd gone into it willingly. I never for a moment thought there was any danger. We none of us did."

And then, when he had eventually become uneasy and gone to look for her, when he had discovered the terrible thing that had happened, he had functioned with the mechanical precision Lucy found so hard to comprehend. He had taken Smith's body to another part of the cellar and concealed it. He had gathered together her few belongings, put them in his father's laboratory —directly above the inner temple—and deliberately started the fire. He had not cared what curious, irreplaceable objects were destroyed: the charms, the manuscripts, the masks, the robes; and Lucy, while appreciating the panic that drove him to do it, could not credit him with the ruthlessness that enabled him to accomplish it. Almost, it seemed, he had been intent on destroying everything tangible that gave meaning to the old man's life; perhaps, in his rage that his father had been driven by magic to the madness of killing to attain his ideal, the destruction did have that symbolic significance.

Then Roland had even, as an added precaution, seen to it that all the copies he possessed of *The Fifth Element* were put into the blaze. Smith's willingness to enter into the playacting passion for secrecy ensured that no one knew of her intention to go to Nine Maidens; Roland's action in removing all trace of her, and of the remotest connection that might point to a reason for her presence in the house, ensured that no one would ever be able to prove she had been there at all.

Chemicals and old, dry timber had made the fire burn furiously. It had blazed down the wooden staircase into the room beneath; unchecked, it would have spread into the house itself in spite of the stout stone walls. But it was checked; Roland saw to that, too. Just as later, when he had privacy and time, he took the body from its hiding place, put it into what was left of the half-collapsed, burned-out inner temple, and sealed it in.

In the softly lit room, silent now, Lucy clung to Roland's hand. Inside her mind she was saying disbelievingly: *You did all that, all by yourself . . .* you, *Roland?* She glanced at Mirabelle, who remained—almost restfully—balanced next to Bunty, her arm lying along the back of the chair. Mirabelle was gazing, without any expression at all, at Henry.

Roland said, "Shouldn't you be writing this down?"

"No," Henry answered curtly. "You'll make your statement to the local police. They'll be here soon."

"Henry," Lucy said. "What will they accuse him of?"

"She means," Mirabelle said, "what will he be charged with?"

"That's up to them. I can't say," Henry said.

"Please," Lucy said. "You must know, you know about these things. He hasn't done anything—anything . . . er . . ." She failed to find the word to qualify Roland's guilt and sat pale-faced and miserable, staring at Henry.

He knew what she was afraid of. His distaste at having anything to do with Roland—even a few words exchanged across a room—did not extend to her. None of it was her fault. "Not murder. If that's what's worrying you."

"What then?" she persisted.

"From what he's said, I should think conspiracy to conceal a body. But I'm not sure. It's a matter for the local police."

"What will happen then?" Roland asked quietly.

"There'll be a post-mortem to establish the cause of death. Then the inquest—"

"But I've told you how she died—poison. It was—"

"I don't care what you've told me. There are legal requirements. . . ."

Post-mortem, inquest, Lucy thought, pushing her mind toward the reality of these things. Henry's face had hardened over whatever strain, whatever grief he was suffering. He was a stranger, cold and official, and she was thankful that he had this barrier of duty to protect himself from their pity. She tried to put herself in his place, to feel what he must be feeling, but she could only be herself and wonder if he hated her as he hated the others.

Roland said to him, "I'm sorry. I'd like you to know I'm sorry for what happened."

As he spoke, there was the sound of car wheels crunching on the gravel drive at the front of the house. Henry turned his head briefly to Roland and with an absolute, controlled contempt, swore at him. Then he went to answer the door.

The noise went on for a long while, at times measured, at times irregular, a muted violence that broke and plunged in the depths of the house. Even when it paused, the silence—torn across by shock—seemed to wrench toward the moment when it would begin again. Or the moment when it would stop completely.

In the kitchen Henry washed his face, dashing cold water against his aching eyes. Stillness seized him. He pressed his hands over his face and in this self-sought darkness he found the image of her, amazingly clear, as the images of those one loves can seldom be summoned: the narrow face, small-featured, with wide-apart eyes, gray as the sea beneath an untidy fair fringe; something in the expression forever untraceably lingering between laughter and perplexity. He had dreamed of her, over and over again: always the same dream of her walking out of the darkness of his sleep to stand beside him with exactly that look, a look that vanished—as dearly as he wished to hold it in his mind—the instant he woke.

He groped for the towel; he was aware of another presence. When he had wiped his face and put the towel down, he saw Mirabelle was there.

"I thought you might like this."

He hesitated, then took the glass of brandy she offered. The liquid spread down his throat with luxurious warmth; it was very good brandy.

"Roland never did all that on his own," he said.

"He is, at this moment, signing his name to the effect that he did."

"He couldn't calculate, think out the moves, plan what had to be done. You could. You're ruthless enough. You knew your father would die before he could be brought to trial; why should any of you go through the squalor and publicity of a scandal for that old lunatic?"

"There'll be that now."

"Oh, you're intelligent enough to know when you're cornered. You'd never have been prepared to compound your guilt with anything rash. When Roland got beyond living with what he knew, he had to be ready to carry the can."

"Perhaps it's evened out the balance at last. There is such a thing as abstract justice." She sat on the kitchen stool, her narrow-limbed body, with its long, flowing look, completely at ease. She seemed to regard him from a world all her own, a world of stillness and certainty, and she reminded him inescapably of another slim, fair-haired woman whose reality now was shattering upon noise and reverberating silences.

"You were afraid, I suppose," she said, "of the way you loved her. Or was it the way she loved you?"

"Be careful what you're saying."

She shrugged. "Why? No . . . I don't suppose anyone's ever said it. Or even guessed. You kept far enough apart from each other. Because you felt it was dangerous to be together? Or because it *might* have been."

Unbelievingly, he heard himself say, "I don't think it would have been. But we both knew. That was enough."

"Enough to keep her anonymous, always in flight."

"How did you know?"

"I know these things sometimes. I've been feeling it in you—"

That was true enough. He had been aware of her clinging to the twists and turns of his mind, just as he was aware, now, of the way his exhausted guilt had gone into her stillness.

"—and I could say that it makes complete sense of her. . . . Only people never do make complete sense, not to each other. At best they move towards a design they can scarcely comprehend, except, perhaps, at the end."

"You can dress up a lot of squalid behavior with sentiments like that; reality excuses nothing. And this is reality—death, the noise down there in the cellar—"

"Her flight, your remorse. And all finished now."

"Are you trying to tell me you believe she was *meant* to come here? To this?"

She spread her hands. "Why anywhere? Why not here, Henry? Why not?"

Then the sounds from below ceased abruptly. In the dreadful, echoing silence, Henry turned his head and looked down the passageway to the open cellar door. Mirabelle touched his arm. "Shall I come down with you?"

"No," Henry said. "No."

23

ON a day of relentless rain, the inquest was opened at the village hall. Being surrounded by matters that threatened to confuse her, Lucy found she could function best by fastening her attention on one thing at a time; it gave some kind of order, if not sense, to events. The police seemed never to be out of the house, never to come to the end of their questions—although as Roland was the only real witness to what had occurred, she could not quite see the point of it all. Their examinations were protracted and minute and threatened to go on forever.

So the inquest was adjourned. It had been opened for the purpose of allowing Henry to state formally that he identified the deceased as his sister. Lucy could not quite see the point of that, either, until she understood that this was part of what Henry had meant about legal requirements: a procedure whereby the coroner could issue a burial order. With an empty, cold feeling in the pit of her stomach, she felt something of Henry's isolation. At least she was with people who shared what was happening to her. Henry, alone in a strange place, had a legal requirement: a slip of paper that allowed him to arrange for the funeral of his sister.

She could not let him go away thinking nobody cared, and she tried to tell him how sorry she was about it all, feeling it was her place to do that.

He said, "I don't blame you for anything, Lucy."

"No, but I want you to know. The others, however much they're sorry . . . if they said so it wouldn't have quite the same meaning. And I don't think you'd be able to believe them . . . because they're so separate from us, so odd."

She said this without apology or accusation, their oddness being now too much of a commonplace in her world to merit much attention. And she knew, as Henry knew, and no one would ever admit, how unrepentantly Mirabelle was lying about her part in the affair. Only Roland could be sure, and he insisted on taking all the blame on himself; Bunty would know, of course, because it was necessary for her to know. The three of them had worked out some kind of balance. As they saw it, justice was not to be found in the impersonal machinery of the law but in their obligations to each other, to the dead woman, the dead magus: a crime had been committed in their midst, someone must pay, someone would pay—and that was the end of it.

"Will you be coming back?" she asked. "For the inquest, the trial?"

"No. It won't be necessary."

"I see. I won't see you again, then. . . ."

"No. I'll think of you, Lucy." It seemed, even as he said it, somehow pointless, a face-saving gallantry; because she needed nothing of him, not even his thoughts.

As if she sensed what he was feeling, she said, "I did need you."

"So Bunty said."

She smiled, shrugging slightly. "Oh, yes . . . she knew. You see, Roland's never been very . . . adequate." She sought for the word without embarrassment but with faint apology—perhaps on her husband's behalf.

Henry had not thought it possible to hold an even lower opinion of Roland, but it was. He remembered the first time he had seen him, walking about in the garden talking to Bunty, shutting Lucy out, right from the start. "You can't mean he doesn't make love to you."

"Not in any satisfactory way; which is far more frustrating than not at all."

He thought this over for a moment before he said, "Thanks. You mean you were desperate."

She smiled again. "Yes. I was desperate. I was ashamed, I thought I was to blame. Somehow, it seemed that the mere fact that I wanted sex was disgusting; it seemed there was nothing I could do except struggle against being a woman. And every day, every night, that woman was being destroyed."

"Lucy . . ."

"Yes. That's the way it was. Not anymore now, because of you; that was why I needed you. That's what you did—you gave me back my respect, my honesty about myself. Please don't be bitter."

Looking at her, he thought only of the wild candor of her body, not of the uneasy, rankling suspicion that he had been led to know it and enjoy it for some purpose. He said, "No, I couldn't be. Not with you."

"Good. I wouldn't want you ever to regret anything either. I never will. You won't, will you?"

"No," he assured her. There was nothing to regret, very little to remember, nothing continuing. He would soon forget her, he thought.

He did think of her when he packed and paid his hotel bill and got into his car to drive through the quiet, abundant morning. The early haze of mist was lifting in the distance, and what he thought was of how she belonged to her surroundings, to the richness of the landscape.

The trees rose about him, making a tunnel of shade through which the sun glinted. They rose from great, grassy banks, their intricate, clutching roots exposed here and there among the tumble of flowers and ferns. Ahead of him, to his left, before a blind corner, there was a break in the banks and the lane opened out to a place wide enough for a car to pull in. He was slowing to change gear, looking toward the corner, when something flickered at the edge of his vision. He braked hard, turning the wheel to the left, bringing the car to a halt half on the lane, half on the spongy leaf mold.

Bunty was standing there. She wore a dress patterned with shadowy green, so much like the dapple of moving leaves he thought that this was what had made her blend into the background—otherwise he would have seen her standing, waiting, as he approached. But still, as he opened the door and she slid into the passenger seat, he said, "Up to your tricks again. It's a way of life with you, I suppose. How did you know I'd come along this lane?"

She smiled and shrugged. She had left the door open and the air was vivid with the sharp, sweet scents of the morning. "I wanted to say good-bye, Henry."

"Good-bye," he said, looking at her. There was an air of quickness about her even as she sat still, hugging her knees, her dress modestly pulled down and wrapped around her legs.

"Ah . . ." she said, and thoughtfully studied her brown little feet, wriggling her painted toenails. "Think kindly of me one day."

"Bunty, bugger off. I've had enough of you and your sort. I've spent sleepless nights trying to see you in real terms, as ordinary people. I can't. In fact, I don't think you exist at all, any of you.

I don't think this *place* exists. It isn't on the map, it isn't in the AA book, it won't be in any gazetteer of the British bloody Isles. Once I've driven away from it, I'll never find my way back, and I'll never want to."

"That's all right," Bunty said, still studying her feet. "Enshrine us in myth. That's what we're *for.* Imagine a policeman having enough poetry in his soul to understand that. . . . But you know what? Part of you will always be here. Always . . . now."

"Policemen don't have souls to have poetry in, or you'd have been out to steal mine, you treacherous little bitch. Lucy said . . ."

Lucy said. There was something Lucy had not said. The clarity of the morning, the gossamer of mist and sunlight filtering between the trees; Bunty's small face half turning toward him, watching as he slowly understood . . . "Lucy's pregnant, isn't she? I've made her pregnant."

"I hope so. Yes. For sure."

"That's what *I* was for. In the wood."

Bunty waited a moment before she answered, "Yes."

"But why Lucy?" he said, and then thought: *Good God, why* not *Lucy?* Ample, generous, loving . . . if ever a woman was built to be an earth mother, it was Lucy. "Why not you? Or Mirabelle?"

"Well, that's our myth, our family myth—that the magus cursed us with barrenness. I don't believe it, I think it just happened. We tried, Mirabelle and I, don't think we didn't try. If one of us could have had a baby, we could have shared— But when I was in my early twenties my periods stopped, no reason, and they just never started again. They won't now; I'm nearly forty. Mirabelle had to have a hysterectomy when she was thirty-eight. But we knew, we *knew* there'd be somebody, special to us, one day. Somebody in the house, a wife, a mother." She gave her plaintive little laugh. "If the magus did curse us, his curse rebounded, on Roland."

"I suppose I do have something to be thankful for: a few hundred years ago, you'd have killed me once I'd served my purpose.

Why didn't Lucy *tell* me?" He was aware of Bunty's sad, knowing eyes, but in spite of himself he could not keep the bitterness out of his voice.

"Because basically she's your sort, Henry . . . respectable, conventional. She knew how you'd react. You'd feel you have some claim—"

"Well, dammit, don't I? It'll be my child. . . ."

"And she's Roland's wife. . . ."

He didn't listen. His mind rushed away with thoughts of how much he had lost, how much he had still to lose if he let himself be cheated. "Roland's going to prison; don't make any mistake about that, you silly little cow. There's nothing you or anyone can do about it. Lucy will be on her own, all by herself in that house . . . where my sister died. Do you think I can just *leave* her there?"

"You must. You're not going to take her away—she wouldn't go. And you can't stay; it isn't your place."

"You mean she doesn't want me."

"That's right. Besides," she added, seeing the look on his face, "she won't be alone. She's got us, Mirabelle and me. And there's nobody here who doesn't wish her well, who won't care for her."

He knew everything she said was true. Lucy had hinted at it, but he'd had no way of understanding then. He turned his head away. There was such a bleakness inside him he wondered what he was doing in this lush, peaceful morning, sitting in his car in a lane where, mysteriously, no one came or went.

"There'd be nothing to stop me—after a time, much later—coming back to see her. . . ."

There was a pause, as if Bunty was thinking about this. She knew what he meant, of course: not just coming back to see Lucy, but to see what sort of a child they'd had. . . .

Will her hair be dark, like mine and Lucy's? Will her eyes be brown, like mine and Lucy's? Why am I so sure, already, it will be a girl?

"Nothing," Bunty said. "Except . . . it would hurt much more,

more than it does now. You wouldn't be able to tell her. And she wouldn't know what you are to her. . . ."

The faintest breath of air, bringing the rich smell of the earth, moved the grasses on the banks and stirred the lacelike fronds of the tall ferns. Henry sat for a while, just looking, not thinking of anything, not thinking that she was right and he would never come back.

She put her hand over his, claiming his attention. He turned to her and said, "No, this isn't my place at all. I've lost too much here."

"But you've given a life. There's that. There'll always be that. . . ."

Death and renewal. The green wheel of the seasons forever turning; stillness and quickening; the ripe ears of corn sprouting through the hollow eye sockets of the skull. . . . All this in the place held in the delicate web of time, haunted by the magic of itself.

Bitterness was like a darkness behind his eyes. He kissed Bunty the way he had always wanted to kiss her, but still the bitterness and darkness were there. He felt her slip away from him, and when he looked she was nowhere to be seen. There were some shreds of grass, crushed by her sandals, on the floor of the car; and on the passenger seat, his pale-blue handkerchief, washed and ironed and neatly folded. He picked it up, tucked it in his pocket, leaned over and shut the door. And drove away.